VICTOR BLACK

BLOOD LEGACY

BY

LEE A.A WOODCOCK PH.D

About the Book

There are a lot of people that don't know about Victor Black. They know he was a local schoolboy adopted by the Whipp family of Twiston, Clitheroe. Some know that he was a timid youth, polite and respectful, but bullied by the Frays growing up.

But what they don't know is that he was born in one of Scotland's most famous chapels, that his bloodline is that of purity. They don't know that he is being silently hunted by The Black Knights, a religious cult dating back to the time of Sir William Wallace as he is believed to be long lost King of Scotland.

But all that is about to change, because Black is introduced to the hidden world of immortality.

Black will do anything to find the long lost Athame's of Maleficus, an ancient set of 13 Witch Blades that if befallen into the wrong hands could wipe out his entire bloodline and create an apocalypse that could cover the world in a second darkness. But as Black gets closer to the truth, he faces an even more dangerous threat.

He just doesn't see it coming.

CONTENTS

BOOK 2______________________________________

MR. LEE A.A WOODCOCK A.A PH.D

BLOOD LEGACY

Victor Black
MMXX

For Leanne, the bright light upon my dark ocean,

and for Zane, the last of our half-dozen …

About the Author:

Lee Woodcock was born in Accrington, Lancashire, and worked for many years as a chartered musculoskeletal specialist physiotherapist. He is a 4th Dan Blackbelt, and former 3 x Heavyweight Gold Medallist British Karate Champion, and World Champion contender. He now lives in Clitheroe with his wife and son, and continues to work in his same profession. However, having completed a *Master of Arts* in English Literature in Creative Writing, he is now well underway with a Ph.D. in the same.

His other books in preparation for publication are *Tom Falcon and the Goblin's Star* and *Blood Legacy II*.

"The Devil's greatest word ever invented to the likes of mankind is 'business' for this is a 'political' word used for legal lies, legal deceit, legal greed, and legal death; it hath no repent for his shackled servants, chiefly those that chose to wield his mighty sword to line their pockets with his silver ..."
Lee. A.A Woodcock

Prologue

My name is Victor Black, and I am dead.

In the name of evil, I have killed many enemies in light of defending this mortal world. It's surreal, truly, because as recompense my wife's throat was slit from ear to ear and my unborn son cut from her belly as if pulled out through a maggot hole.

I was born on the hard stone flags of St. Margaret's Chapel, my birth set deep within the high walled outcrop of Edinburgh Castle. The Chapel, from my grasping, was built in the year 1130 BC by *King David I (b. 1084)* in memory of his mother, Queen Margaret (1046-1093 CE) for her devout practices of Roman Catholicism in her new adoptive home-lands: *Scotland*. It was here Margaret provided aid and care to the poor in mass quantities; however, it was only in later years to come, 1250 BC (*thereabouts*) that Queen Margaret was sanctified by the Roman Catholic Church and bestowed with the title of 'Saint Margaret', by Pope Innocent IV. It was there upon that freezing November night that I was placed upon the room's high presbytery and left to die.

Apart from the blooded alter shroud swaddling me at the time of my discovery, its golden embroidered crucifix charred blood red, I have no evidence to this day of my ancestral lineage. Though I have, however, been back many times as a man to see my rightful birthplace in search of truth, but I can honestly say, there is nothing that I have found. Like many others with the name, *Margaret*, my visits have always been under the guise on St Margaret's Day, to pay homage to my homely kin. I kiss gentle the hand of the Saint to thank her on that fateful night for watching over me. *Does she hold the secret to my past?* The chapel, its oblong circumference only small, is situated on a rocky mound inside the walls of the castle. Ornately embossed with figurines of blue, purple, green and red in sparkling psychedelic-stained glass windows, it was originally etched by Douglas Strachan in 1922, each of which depicts four noble Scottish saints: St. Andrew, St. Columba, St Margaret, St. Ninian, along with the prominent, Sir William Wallace.

Why the talk on St. Margaret's Chapel? It's simple: first, I catch my breath as I reminisce to tell you a tale. I believe it is imperative for any man (or woman) to know their ancestral lineage, their place of birth – to look upon the doorway on how *they* came into this world – all of which, in time, may reveal to them many unseen answers.

This is a true story. Victor Black is not my real name.

I was born an orphan which was fact. I was given no name, and made nameless, apart from 'Chapel Boy' in hearsay, as bestowed unto me by the other kids in the orphanage. After fruitless searches by local authorities for any link of my parentage, it brought back no trace of any evidence whatsoever. They said, *"They had exhausted every avenue"*, where I was further told, *"It was a costly enquiry"*. Then there was also the part about me living in fear of my life. They said that I had gathered a religious following: *'The Fellowship of Black Knights'* – a religious cult whom prophesised the return of the monarchy to Scotland. The media didn't help either. They created a snowstorm of propaganda headlines: *The Shrouded Boy of Christ* and *The Reborn King*, along with other defamatory tones: *Gods Rejected Disciple* and *Sir William Wallace's Bane.*

To this day I care not of my maternal mother's whereabouts. Though at four years old, the politics involved in this clandestine search were very little understood for me. As I now sit and write, cold shivers crack my spine as I cross into the realms of dark remembrance.

The people I have shot, the throats I have ripped out, the people I have fed upon, and for what? Their souls rip at my virtuosity with each fleeting thought of their death. I am haunted. *Literally.* I will never escape their screams. I'm reminded never to make contact with Scotland again, and to *never* seek out the Stone of Scone. That should I fail my next mission, or flout my orders, or disobey my commands; they will kill my son outright in cold blood - the son I have never met, the son snatched from my dead wife's womb.

It was an eye for an eye, a tooth for a tooth, they declared. *It was blood war.*

Some would agree, no doubt. Do I care what people think of me? Right now, this very second? I wish I could take every single kill back, and fuck the uniformed bourgeois, but it's far too late for that now. I'm in it up to my middle, so call me what you will: sniper, murderer, cold blooded assassin, hunter in the night. Let's face facts. I *am* a killer. I was trained to kill.

The bourbon I coldly sip as I recite these lines burns my tongue, twanging the back of my throat. *Am I a drunk?* The heat of the log burner scalds my face in such a way it warms my silent tears, melting the ink in my pen, the flash of red fire in my eyes. There is a tightening in my chest, my lips whiten, the air chords in my throat choke me, my mind, and senses now locked in. *How the hell have I ended up in this position?* They have tried to silence me. I did not listen. I will never listen. *What on earth have I done so wrong in life for God to abandon me? I followed orders. I shot to kill. I ripped out my enemy's throats. I was told I was saving England. I was born in his Holy House for fuck sake.* I stare into the dark abyss as firelight embers of orange tinder flash over my gaze. *Have I missed anything?* I don't have the answers.

Actually, I don't give a fuck …

* CHAPTER 1*

~ The Midnight Express ~

It was a white crisp November's day, the icy chill forged icicle patterns on the blistering glass of my dormitory window. I could see them twinkling brightly from my bunk as a slice of uncut yellow sunlight streamed in to warm my face. The harder I looked, the swirls of blue-ice became evermore mesmerising. I remember that day well. Nobody knew it, but that day was my birthday. I was four. I went to the library early that morning in search of my favourite book. They say favour fortunes the bald, though honestly, I didn't see it coming. It was a strange day, nonetheless, and time seemed to fly, and after a hearty supper I was in bed early, excited to read my book. It was freezing, literally, where being in bed back then was one of the warmest places in the orphanage. In fact, as I looked round, we were all in bed, though only a scant of us was reading, the rest fast asleep. It was dark by 4pm, and I always read by torchlight. Our elders would leave torches near to our beds. The last they wanted were pissy beds in the morning. At least with a torch we could find our way to the bathroom during the dark night, though some pissed the bed on purpose. A lot of us were shit scared of the dark, and also of our elders.

The Witches by Roald Dahl always sparked my imagination. I was at least halfway through the book, but I must've fallen asleep. That was when it happened. All I remember is being pulled feet first out from the bottom of my bed. I was held down as a sock was shoved in my mouth smoothed over by a strip of thick tape. It was the big hands that grabbed me. They squeezed my arms, and my throat, and bound my hands tightly. There were two of them. They hung me upside down by my ankles and lowered me quickly into a hessian sack. The next I remember is the sound of the closing of a car boot, then the smell of diesel, and the sound of a car engine, and the long hissing of steam engines. Then it was the screeching of whistles from the platform controller's echoing in my ears. Then I heard them talk - the deep voices of two Scottish men.

"*Stay away from bonnie Scotland ya little cunt*", a perpetual threat that has lasted all my life. I kicked, I yelled, I punched. "*If we catch ya here, you'll feel our wrath,*" they added as a parting shot. I felt very afraid.

The smell of dusty black coal bolstered my nostrils as it clogged my airways. I was drowning in dirt. Then it was my eyes, my tiny eyes. The silver-sharp speckled particles pierced the blue of my eyes as though it tiny shards of splintered glass. Light spilled in and down through the tiny square holes in the sack. Quickly I flicked my lids to clear my vision, but it didn't work. It made them worse. *I canny see.* They began to smart, and then water. Then I heard the click of the boot, I felt my tiny body rise up and sail through the air. My breathing quickened. I thought I was never going to land. I inhaled a final breath ready for impact, but the landing never came.

It was strange. I was running bare foot, the white of the moon to my east, the trees, their branches bare, their mighty bows like tall black spikes shooting up out of the forest floor. I was naked, but I was not cold. Ice was on the ground; the smell of fresh blood was in the air.

I'm not sure how long I was out cold, because I was shook vigorously awake. I felt the sting of the tape rip off my mouth, the dry sock yanked out. They untied my hands.

I feel like I'm going to have a heart attack. I fall down onto all fours and threw up violently, all over someone's black shiny shoes.

Pat. Pat. Pat, went a big hand upon my back.

I was face to face with last night's supper, beans on toast. 'I can'ee breath!' I exclaimed, *Cough. Cough.* Black coal streamed from both my nostrils; streaky white phlegm covered with black shards slid out my mouth as though it a large slimy slug. The sharp glass-like particles sliced my gums as I bit down hard to absorb the pain from my chest. It was on fire. I was yanked bolt upright, my back patted fiercer until the colour in my cheeks ran pink. I began to breathe easier, my vision returning. I soon look up to find the owner of the shoes.

"W-where a-am i?" *Cough. Cough.*

A shadow of what appeared to be a big man stood towering above me. To my left, adjacent to some huge doors were what looked like square wooden pigeonholes from floor to ceiling. Inside the holes they were crammed with brown and white envelopes of all sizes. Further down to the back there were huge, hefty brown sacks stacked, un-opened. *Was I on a train?* A cup of tea was shoved quickly beneath my nose, a tad shy of hot. *Did he want me to drink this?* I did not hesitate. The cup was big, my hands tiny to its huge elaborate handle. I look up again, my vision a little better. I squinted. *Who was this man?* He was still all a blur. I swear to God I was going to die. I shook violently, but not because of the cold, it was purely out of fear. The knots in my gut twisted and pulled like deep rooted vines.

The man was smartly dressed in dark blue, pin-striped shirt in sky-blue, matching waistcoat and mailman hat. Contentedly he sat me on a small wooden stool to steady me. He brushed the lose particles of coal from my pyjamas. Then, turning his back to me, from out of another bag he pulled out a pair of old black shoes, a white shirt that had gone grey, a pair of grey trousers with a hole in the left knee and an old brown duffle coat. As I looked harder, I could see a couple of its wooden shiny buttons amiss. I felt as though these garments had already been readied for me.

"Who are you?" I asked, but again, no reply came. The man just stared at me stone faced. "I have nee quarrel with you," I stated, but it made little difference. Then the man smiled, then calmly sighed as his vision bore into me as I took a deep sip of my tea. *What was this man thinking?* I began to wretch, again, my lungs felt as though they were burning with ice. But my eyes – they continued to sting as though pepper sprayed with a hundred wasps.

The man never spoke a word. Not one. He carefully helped me dress into the new clothes. Then, when done, he reached over to where his cup of tea was positioned on his desk, brought back a white porcelain dish, where in the middle of it were two slices of white bread, its centre packed with delicious filling. I could smell it. He broke off some of his sandwich and handed it to me. I'd never tasted anything so delicious: ham and cheese and pickle, the bread was thick cut, laced with proper butter and a smidgen of mustard. I loved food; except I didn't ever seem to get enough of it. Once I had liver and onions. It cost the orphanage a lot of money. It was all we could afford one Christmas, instead of turkey. This was like that for me, it tasted so good. I glared at my food. I struggled to hold it, but there was no way I was letting this beast go. I was like a dog with a bone.

"Thank you," I said. I smile as he sees me eat; in fact, he encouraged with a gentle gesture of his hand. He smiles and nods. He too takes a bite of his sandwich, his teeth pristine and white.

"Thank you", I repeated again. I was so so hungry.

The mailman wore a wedding ring, a single band of gold. I like to think perhaps he too had children of his own. As I look down to lift my food to my mouth, I notice a brown paper tag hanging low about my neck – it was blank. *Where the hell did that come from?* Keeping it there was a thin cord of white rope. I took it in my stride as part of my attire and said nothing. After all, I didn't really know this chap, and the last I wanted was to upset him. I knew what it was like dealing with strangers. They were unpredictable. I watched in awe as he moved about the carriage, rummaging. Then he gave me on old worn leather satchel, and in there he placed my dusty pyjamas then fastened it firmly. He reached inside the left pocket of his inside waistcoat and pulled out a round silver watch on a long matching chain. It shone a bright gleam against the lights of the carriage as he checked the time. Upon its lid there was an inscription scribed of old, written in fancy writing, possibly Latin, though it was hard to make out. I tried to look again but it was difficult with the dim carriage lights. Perhaps it was a gift he had been given, a gut instinct maybe due to its well kempt opulence. I had no real idea what time it was, though faint daylight spilled in through the high slit-windows of the train. Then from out his jacket he pulled out a pristine white handkerchief. He unfolded it delicately then dabbed a corner of it on his tongue to wet it. Reaching out he held my chin firmly with one hand, then began to clean my face with the other. The initials on the handkerchief were stitched in blue: *RVW*. After that he cleaned over my black dusty eyes too, leaning me back as if in a barber's chair then pouring fresh warm water from his nearside flask into my eyes. He then began to comb my hair, though his hair was greying. His nose seemed a little different, cut with a high ridge like the small hump on a bridge, as if it had been broken at least twice. In seconds he primed a left parting on my head, and smartened me up. As he leant over me making me look lived in his name tag spilled out from beneath his waistcoat: *Victor*. I wasn't a great reader, though I easily read that. All I did at my former orphanage was read; I was always in the library, tucked in some dark corner reading, but mostly keeping out of harm's way. "…out of sight, out of mind." That's what I liked to think. As mostly I read at night in bed by torchlight so I wouldn't wake any of the other boys in my dormitory. It was much safer to be in bed, except that night it wasn't. All I had growing up were books. They were my friends, the characters within them, as you didn't make friends in my orphanage. Not a chance. And if someone did want to be your friend, you always questioned their motives. It was first up best dressed in my world, and if you weren't first up, it also meant no food, let alone no shoes or socks.

As I sat with Victor the air around us cushioned with a backdrop of comfortable silence. The clicks of the wheels of the rickety old train rolled over the tracks, white steam flowing past the high windows of the carriage. My eyes were better now, though it took a while for them to adjust. The water poured into them certainly helped. We slurped our tea, him checking persistently his watch, more so as the train eventually came to a slow, and then to a hissing halt. Victor stood up sharply. I took a last bite of my sandwich, just in case. *What was happening now?* I hadn't finished my food yet. Afterall it was a big butty.

"Mr. Conductor what's happening now?"

In a hurry he took back my unfinished mug. I wiped the back of my hand on my sleeve. On then went my coat as he buttoned it to the top. Then, over my shoulder, he threw my leather satchel, yanking it firmly down. I remember it smelt old, as if mouldy. I found there was a delicacy of etiquette that overshadowed this man's demeanour. He knelt in front of me, a glare of blue-on-blue shimmering into my eyes. He gave a subtle wink and smiled. Then slowly, as if methodical, he leant into his breast pocket and pulled out a pen. An idea seemed to flash in his mind. I could see it. He grabbed my tag, where on my label he wrote in capital letters:

BLACK.

There was a distinct rasp upon the mail carriage door. *Who was that?* Victor hurried me to its entrance then slid the heavy oily doors apart. He looked distinctly left then right. The bright light of the outside struck me head on. It was snowing; white droplets of pure ice beat down upon my brow. Then, with one final swoop I was pulled off the train by another strange man. *Who the hell was this?* I thought. As I glimpsed back the carriage doors closed shut. The Victor I had gotten to know disappeared in a puff of smoke as the train hissed off into the far distance.

Where in the hell was I now?

* CHAPTER 2*

~ Clitheroe Town ~

The new man jostled me in and out of crowds on the platform. The shoes on my feet felt like flip-flops. I shook wet sleet from my hair. I felt like a lost dog, the paper tag around my neck flapping in the snowy wind, whipping me in the face like the tail of a small dragon. And to top it all off, the people here spoke funny. They didn't seem to have an accent at all, unlike me. I was glad my coat was buttoned all the way up. I could feel droplets here and there of stray snowflakes slip down the back of my neck. The weather was iced cold. I clamped my jaw tight shut, and though I didn't show it, I was very afraid of this man.

"Keep still", he barked as he persistently yanked at my arm. "Do as you're told." He repeated, "or you'll get a clip!"

"Y-yes, Sir." I had to comply.

A trilby hat rested upon his head, a long grey mac covering his back, black shiny shoes upon his feet. He smoked a thin wooden pipe - I could smell the tobacco on his clothes, and could see the arse end of the black pipe sticking out of his lower pocket. He was a thin sort of fellow with a wiry nose, clean shaven, brown tie and white shirt. The whitest I've ever seen a shirt. Whether through fear, or for some other reason, I felt my senses up a gear to high alert. The guy's accent was posh, and before I knew it, he had steered me through the station and out into the open street. As I quickly glimpsed there was a row of neatly parked police cars, each officer in each car turning their vision in my direction. *Was I being arrested?*

"Get your head down." The man pushed my head down hard. I felt my neck crack at the base of my skull. "I said, best do as you're told, lad."

My feet were striding at least three to his one. A door opened. He bungled me into the back of black Mercedes. I felt a hammering in my chest, my ribcage was about to burst. The diesel fumes from the exhaust shot up my nose, burning my airways. The pupils in my eyes became dilated, and throbbed in sinus rhythm with each beat of my throbbing heart. Then it was other hearts I could hear too? *Wasn't it?* As my eyes sharply flitted about, making sense of my bearings, there were two other men sat in the front of the car. They were in suits, possibly undercover cops as this car were teeming with radios. Amidst the unbridled animosity an open ashtray lay in the front filled with thick backlogs of dead cigarette butts all orange end up. The interior of the roof was stained in dark yellow with old smoke. I should know … I was led on my back staring up at it, the leather satchel strap choking my air tubes as he pinned me down.

"Stay fucking still!" barked the man a third time. "… or woe betide you, boy. I'll not tell you again!" He raised his hand to hit me with the back of it.

"I-i s-sir," I timidly replied. *I didn't dare move.*

The guy in the back leant forwards to the two men in the front. "Go to the rendezvous point. Now!"

"Yes Boss," one said.

We drove for what seemed like a short time. The sky was blistering white with snow, the car tyres slushed on the open road. I could see, hear, taste and smell everything around me, along with feel every bump beneath the tyres of the car, every stop and every start, every turn in the road.

It didn't take long until we came to a halt on a gravelly car park in what seemed the middle of nowhere. At first the car drove around in circles, as if unsure, then, all of a sudden, it skidded to a halt.

'We're here,' said the driver.

The back door of the car burst wide open. "Out yer little twat!" ordered the man in the trilby.

I struggled to flip over and find my feet. "I'm coming", I replied in haste, but with no patience the man dragged me by my satchel. Now I had a hole in my other trouser leg as I fell onto my knees in the dirt and mud and bust my bottom lip. Cold ice and water and gravel entered my mouth.

"Get up!", the man ordered. "Yer little *shit!*"

"I-I, S-sir".

I glared about as best as I could. Then I saw it in the distance. It was far off to the East, poking up through the mist. It was a big hill. Through a long cutting in the tall green trees it called out to me – as if I knew it. It whispered to me. Pure white snow covered it from top to bottom in a snug blanket, the soft snow that clumps together easily as you firmly make a snowball; its picturesque views, some of its lower parts bright green and deep auburn, with parting long walls like the pillars in Rome that ran superiorly up its banks, separating its lush grassy meadows. In a flash all my fear had left me. I felt I was home: *Scotland*, its deep Glens, roughhewn grass, a place where I was once free.

The man in the trilby leant forwards and pointed his bony finger in my face. "Be good, boy."

"Y-yes Sir."

I watched as he got back into his car, nodding at the new man that had just grabbed my arm. No words were spoken between either of them, but their gestures said it all.

"You're with me now", said the new man, but before the black Merc left the car park, he asked me to stand still a moment whilst he went over to the man in the trilby. *He must've forgotten something, perhaps?* Except, as I look on, I care not to mention what he did to that man. He wasn't gone long. Then the new man in the car park came back to me, a casual walk about his attire. He seemed relaxed, as if without a care in the world. I watched as the black Merc sped off, skidding aggressively in the snow.

"Are you well?' said he.

I looked up. I adjusted my satchel. It was burning the hell out of the skin on my neck. The thick coat about me was bothering me. I felt flustered. It was like I was wrapped in a quilt, like a pastry sausage roll. I took a deep breath and forgot about what had just happened. Now, I had to concentrate on where I was and whom I was with. I brushed the slush from my clothes. I could feel a thin river of blood trickling down my leg from inside my trousers. I didn't want any fuss, so I said little over the matter. *What was that smell?* It smelt like food far off in the distance.

"Are you well?" the man asked again. He lifted my trouser leg and dabbed it with some tissue from his pocket. *How did he know I was bleeding? Did he smell the blood like I did?* It smelt sweet to me, as if it a nectarine of jam and honey and cream, with a tad of fresh liver.

"It's just a scratch. I've had worse," I said.

"So, you're a tough guy eh?" The man went on. "How was your trip?' He wore blue jeans and blue gilet, a blue baseball cap with the letters NY imprinted in gold at its front covering his head.

"It was dusty", I replied. "I've never seen as many envelopes in my whole life."

The man gave a slight chuckle to himself. He walked me back to his car – a green Cherokee Jeep. He sat me high on the back seat, removing my satchel, placing the seatbelt over my shoulder. I sat behind the driver's seat. I distinctly remember its tyres being huge, thick and black and knobbly and easily as tall as me. Sat in the front was a lady dressed in a brown fur coat, red dress. As I looked subtle cat-flick spectacles lined level with her eyebrows rested over her calm face. I still remember the distinct smell of her perfume: *Chanel No. 5.* The man got into the car to drive, then turned to face the back.

"I'm Robert,' he said, 'and this is Ida."

We glared hard at each other. It was them against me. My mind raced. I rubbed my eyes a final time, giving me time to think. *What shall I say? Perhaps I should make a run for it?* Then it came to me.

"I had a mug of tea on a train. I ate a sandwich, and it burnt my tongue. But I liked it very much." It was all I could think of to say. I didn't want to mention the coal sack just in case they were going to put me back in it. *Where in hell was I?*

"Is that so?" Ida seemed calm. They laughed a little, and then came the questions.

"What's your name?" asked Robert. "I see you've got *BLACK* written on your I.D Label." As he said this Ida reached forwards and removed the chord from my neck. "What Robert is trying to say is what is your first name, Master Black?" continued Ida, and though I didn't have a name, it just came out.

"Victor," I said. "Victor Black." If I didn't give him a name what then? Maybe he'd choke me with my satchel too, or shove my face into the slush outside, or crack me on my head with the back of his hand. That was the last I wanted.

"Victor, eh?" replied Robert. "I have a friend called; Victor ..." Robert switched on the Jeep's ignition. The engine sparked into life, and we began to move off.

"Welcome to Clitheroe, Victor," said Ida. "You'll be staying with us for a while. You'll have your own room. You'll have three square meals a day and a hot bath every evening before bed. You will learn your English and your mathematics, and you will attend the local school: Pendle Hill Comprehensive. You will attend Church every Sunday with us as a family and you will learn your Hymns. Once a week you will do your chores; change your bedding, hoover your room, dust your shelves. Is that understood?"

I kept my chin up. I did not delay. I'd been asked questions before back at my orphanage, and when I didn't answer immediately, I got a clout by my elders. Once I got hit so hard I was knocked on the hall floor, and my left ear whistled for a week. That was when I first got my first taste of blood. My ear bled for days. All I could do was dab it with tissue. "Yes, Ida," I replied respectfully. The thought of church didn't go down well, but the sound of having my own room and three-square meals a day lifted my spirits immensely. The one thing about being at the orphanage was I always felt hungry.

Ida smiled. "Good." I think she was a mind reader. "You'll not go hungry in our house. The Lord provides." Ida said. I felt taken aback.

As we drove, I glared out to my East. I couldn't take my eyes off it. Against the horizon in blistering snow, it was monstrous, yet so inviting. I wanted to climb its mighty banks; I could smell the fresh watery grass despite the dense white mists surrounding its borders. This huge mound of earth reached up to the grey heavens. It certainly left its distinct mark upon the bleak horizon. I followed it as we drove for what seemed like an age. No matter where we drove it could always be seen. And to see it gave me comfort, for it continued to whisper to me, calling my name. Then we stopped dead.

"We're here, Victor."

"We are?" I said. "Where is here?"

"Home," replied Robert.

Ida opened my side of the car door. I didn't even realise where we were, or how we had gotten here. I felt all in a daze. I was so tired. I looked up. It was a house, a white house, made of stone, a huge golden thatched roof rested thickly atop its lofty brickwork. I glanced back over my shoulder. *Was I being watched?* The drive up to the house was long and very gravelly, tall trees overshadowing its route, a thick stone wall surrounding its borders. Evenly spaced every few hundred yards white gates were sunk back into the walls. Old leaded windows from the house shouted out with magnificent colours of blues and greens and yellows and reds as the sunlight broke through up onto its solitary icy panes.

"This way, Victor," Ida led the way, my hand in hers. I'll never forget that day. In we walked, the halls and stairwells carpeted. There was a smell, a fragrant smell of deep pine, much like the woodland realms of Scotland that lay idle to the rear of my orphanage. There were lots of rooms to my left and right. I was lead straight into the study, where I was told to take off my shoes and coat, and to make myself at home, to wait on the sofa whilst Ida would make me and Robert a hot drink and a bacon sandwich. I sat comfortably a while, glaring about my new surroundings.

In The Study there was another door at the far back of the room. It was a wooden door, thick and heavy, with a huge brass handle. Robert walked to it and opened it with a key from his pocket. He gestured for me to come, so I did, willingly.

"This is where I do all my work, Victor."

I glared about in awe. From top to bottom bookshelves lined the walls. The titles now when I reminisce were of the following: Law, Psychology, Anatomy and Physiology, Sociology, Archaeology, Anthropology, Business, Economics, Mathematics, Astronomy – simply far too many to mention. There was certainly no Roald Dhal, not good at all. Then I pointed to an object resting on the wall high above the fireplace. Robert saw me and smiled. It was boxed off in a thin glass case. It had a large round handle, its hilt glittered as if with blue diamonds and red jewels, its black blade sparkled in the sunlight as it broke through into the room, flashing as though alive. There was an inscription on the blade scribed in gold, much the same as the writing on Victor's pocket watch. I looked again. It *was* the same. I know that now to be Latin:

Cum mortem venit vita … (With death comes life…).

I had to ask. "What is that Mr. Robert?"

He paused a short while. He stood and walked over to the frame set high up on the wall. "That, Victor, is one of the Athame's of Maleficus. It is said that the glass surrounding it is magical, coveted with a spell to protect the blade from other worldly elements."

"It's truly magnificent," I said.

"That's a big word," replied Robert, obviously inspired, I guess. But I was in awe. He turned then pulled a very old book off his shelf. The binding was fragile, its front tarnished. Its title was: *Ancient Artefacts of English Witchcraft by Olus Nider.* It was dated 1598. Robert seemed to hold the book with such delicacy as if it a new-born baby.

He slowly flicked to the page he wanted. Within moments he found a picture of the exact same blade.

"Look!" He pointed to the picture. And I gazed with enthusiasm. "There are another twelve in existence – besides this one." He said. It looked the same, except its handle was a little different, and the length of its helm a little shorter. But still, the writing on the blade read the exact same.

"Amazing, Mr Robert." I was genuinely intrigued. Though I knew it was a blade of sorts, of course, and it was probably deathly sharp, but there was one word that stood out to me. "What's *Malc – ift – cuss*". I asked. I was unable to pronounce the word.

"It's Latin, but in English, it's otherwise known of as: *The Black Witch Blade,*" said Robert.

"Witch?" I felt a sense of excitement run through me. I jumped up for joy and moved closer for a better look. Robert lifted me up. "You mean like, like, like - *The Witches* from *Road Dahl*? That sort of Witch, Mr Robert?" I couldn't believe I was living in a house with a real witch blade on the wall. To look at it head on its blade at the front point of its axis was criss-crossed, as if in the shape of a + sign, but with a deeper vertical length. I couldn't take my eyes off it. "Can I hold it, Mr Robert, please Sir?"

"Wouldn't we all like to hold it, Victor" His eyes seemed to flash when he gazed at it in return. "… except, the only way to get it out to hold it would be to break the glass. Its permanently sealed. I have tried many times and am in fear of damaging it. It's been sealed airtight for centuries; to protect the blade and sheath from anything external that may damage its surface such as damp air, salt, or wind. It is very old indeed, Victor. It has been in my family for generations and is the heirloom of my histories.

"It's truly beautiful," I replied. Its sheer splendour, to look upon its being, felt completely magical. Then he said something that took me back, though elated that I was.

"Someday, this will be yours, Victor."

"M-mine?" I felt my eyes glean over.

"Yes. Yours. And yours alone."

"Really?" ... *was I hearing him, right?* I glared at it, as if for hours, its hilt sparkled brightly, and Robert saw me, and he smiled intently. I felt mesmerised. In fact, for the first time in my life, I felt like I was home. And what affirmed that feeling for me was when I was shown my bedroom. Immediately, I saw a bookshelf (my new bookshelf). It wasn't as big as Mr Roberts, or the one at the orphanage, but there on the shelf the full collection of Roald Dhal rested, along with C.S Lewis, The Hobbit, and another three books by the same author, J.R.R Tolkien: *The Lord of the Rings.* I gratefully fell to my knees and opened some of their pages, smelling them with my nose. Mind you, some of the words I did not understand, let alone have the ability to read, let alone pronounce. But as I studied the pictures on the front covers and let my mind wander with content, I heard a whisper – *again.* It was ever so soft. It called to me. Where was Robert? He had gone. So, I strolled over to my bedroom window and peered out. *Was it Robert in the garden, or Ida on the landing?* I walked to the landing and back, but no one was there. Then I heard it again; it was a faint whisper, like the slightest breeze upon the wind rustling the last remaining autumn leaves before they fall from the trees. I looked again, this time I saw it and smiled.

"Hello", I said, and I waved, though abashed. And it moved, as though a large hand was stroking its back as if it a sleeping dragon. I waved again.

It smiled back. It was staring at me. Its mighty

shoulders an emblem of immense power - its face peering in through my window. It told me that I was home. And I believed it, too. I felt it inside me, and a faint warmth in my chest gathered. I glared at it, inspired. It was huge and green, and red in certain parts. I could smell it on the wind, and I know that hill today to be Pendle Hill, and from that day onward, Clitheroe was my home.

* CHAPTER 3*
~ High School ~

I won't beat about the bush. Like some growing up through school I was bullied. No matter what your accent, ethnicity, religious beliefs, or your colour of skin - some kids know none of that allegory bullshit. Their brains aren't equipped to deal with such human diversity created in a corrupt world by adult politics. *How can it be?* That's what I always thought. Most know nothing about life. Think about it? We're all born with a clean slate, an empty cup, as they say. All they see at that time is 'indifference', felt through primal instinct of emotional displaced turmoil, or perhaps overshadowed by negative peer relations, rejection, or abuse stemming from home. What I'm trying to illustrate here is, they have their reasons, like a lot of adults too, I guess.

I was bullied at High School, persistently, but more so by one boy in particular: *Ivan Vray.*

At the time I remember thinking *why am I so scared of this boy? Why was it me he picked on? Why did he hate me so much? ...* In hindsight I showed him the necessary fear he needed in order for him to persistently continue to taunt me. It was a fear I showed to him time and time again that made him feel powerful about his own broken ego. For him, my weakness was his emotional addiction, and for that, I paid the price thrice over. I feared going into school most days, particularly in my final year. That was when it was at its worst. At times I played truant. I feared seeing the boy. I'd get violently sick and throw up, and then when my friends would ask what the matter was, I'd tell them *I ate something that didn't agree with me.* Then there were those that socialised with him – his *lackeys.* Even after spending days at a time self-isolating, it was a difficult habit to break. I was a pent-up sheepdog, chewing my own legs off to escape the chains in my kennel.

I won't lie; life at the very beginning was hard for me in England. Though its lush green valleys reminisced in silence with the winds, a summers haze flouting over its wide lands, deep down I resented the place, no matter how pretty its lands. *What the fuck was I doing here in this shithole?* To Ivan I was a positive polarity. Even in the dinner queue I would try not to make eye contact with him. He'd snigger, and whisper, with the odd time I'd feel stray strands of spaghetti hoops land upon my back, or on my head. Once a loose string fell upon my face. It dangled there, looking all spaghetti-like as if it a small squid, its tentacles creeping over my cheeks looking for a foothold inside my nostrils. I was so embarrassed. The full dining hall broke out into fits of laughter. Other days I'd get my dinner, find a seat in the canteen, glare at it as though it was alien, then bin it. I must've put hundreds of pounds in the bin that year. The company I kept in a select few friends at the beginning was humble, though I'd sit there quietly, wondering why the hell I was born. No wonder there are kids out there committing suicide today. Same for adults, too. *Why me?* That is the key question, isn't it? "ME!" *Is it you?*

In attempts to cheer me up my father would tell me stories of his father Robert Senior, champion bare knuckle fighter, former Royal Military Police. He'd sympathise, and say,

"Victor... being bullied is what happens to almost every child at some point in their lives. Some more than others. But what's important is how they react to that person's negative demeanour? Do they cower by allowing self-pity to overshadow their day? Or do they take hold and make positive changes that prevent such unfortunate events from being continued?"

What the hell was he trying to say?

The story of Robert Snr was always inspiring. When I was first told it I would shadow box in my room just off the back of its extravagance, and that of his popularity in Clitheroe. As a family we would watch the boxing on TV. Bob was well respected. *That's how I wanted to be. Was that even at all possible?* I wanted to be *him*, it gave me hope. But in the end it did not give me one ounce of courage to fight. I had come to the solemn conclusion that fighting wasn't really my thing. It made me shake inside. I hated confrontation, much like *George McFly* from Back to the Future. I had to admit it. I was a full-blown coward. The incentive to even get dressed in the mornings was like walking to the river's edge for a pale of water while its banks were riddled with hungry crocodiles. Often, they would snap, bleeding my skin. Sunday nights were the worst. Even the word 'Sunday' meant dread. Going to church wasn't a problem anymore compared to school.

At home I'd be quiet. Really, I was oppressed. The delicacy of my emotional state was twisted as though thorny dead bracken choked the remits of my sanity. It was indeed plagued. The spikes of my moods were just as ambivalent. I didn't even seek solace in conversation anymore. Not with anyone. I mean, I didn't even talk to myself anymore, and that was saying something. The older I became, the more I understood, the more I anticipated, and the more I hated my existence. Just being 'present' in the image of ones weakened self was daunting enough. I felt de-humanised, de-masculinised. I had a tenant living inside my head rent free, and though I was the Landlord, fuck the rent. Thinking about it again, he was a squatter. A dirty squatter with more rights than me. That's right. Even a court order couldn't get the fucker out. His negative presence trailing amidst the backdrop of my vision alone was enough to throw me off the edge of Witch Quarry in Twiston. He was there when I opened my books at school. He was there when I was eating my tea at home. He was even there when I was taking a shit. Then it was the eyes. Lots of eyes in school staring, glaring, all fixated on me. *Was I paranoid? Yes, the fuck I was.* I didn't know who my friends were anymore. In fact, I didn't have any. I think being with me alone was guilty by association. People got the message. To be seen with me was death to all. *Vive la France!* I was unobtrusive to all. This whole process was unsocial, political, and substantially time consuming to my overheated brain. I was spat on. I was belittled. I was punched. Inside my spirit was broken. I was isolated and violated. I was persecuted, even in my absence I was made guilty for a crime I did not commit. For four long years I had tolerated the physical abuse, the silent abuse, the unseen abuse, along with the mental abuse (both seen and unseen by my peers). But my final year at school was the worst of all. The teachers did nothing, except turn a blind eye. Why, because they didn't give a shit. They didn't need the extra paperwork. Not only that - but their senses were also dimmed to such hidden atrocities probably because they had their own shit to deal with at home. The older I became the more aggressive Ivan became. And though I trudged through shit and mud and piss to reach the end of school, God only knows how the fuck I did it. In truth: I had no option but to stay home for fear of reprisal. Hence, out a negative came a positive. I was forced to study – and that appeared to work for me. I was given the time and space to breath. It allowed me to adopt a fresh outlook on life. I had become better at ducking and diving. This allowed me, inside my mind and my spirit, to heal. I felt like a blue orchid, about to blossom. I discovered isolation became my only friend, my strongest ally, my only endeavour to oppose those that oppress us, and succeed. *It was me, myself, and I.* I knew that now. I began to learn to hate failure. *I began to learn to hate my fucking squatter.* The way I'd worked it out. If my brain was busy working for me, then it wasn't busy thinking of him. I'd run up Pendle Hill. I purchased an 'at home' multi-gym. Press ups and sit ups on the top of Pendle; rain, sleet, snow, pissing down rain. This guy had fucked me right off. I was angry. I was that angry that inside I was ripping with rage. And as time went on, the last remaining year at school flew by. In the end it was 'exactly' as my father had said, *I had learnt how to react to that person's negative demeanour. That pent up aggression, that sheepdog inside me chewing at my rope; except, now that dog was now loose.*

They say things happen for a reason. That's how I see it now.

But in all, it wasn't until my 19th birthday that fate had other plans for me. On that night I was home on leave in Clitheroe from York St John College. I was 6ft 4inch, athletic build, and well spoken. I was at university studying to be an Anthropologist. It was my first year. The human body completely inspired me, along with digging up old bones, old fossils, old bottles and pottery. It endorsed my character and offered the promise of a lifetime career whilst covered in shit.

That, however, was all about to change.

That night I had gone to a local pub in the town to meet with old friends. It was a Saturday. public house near to the town clock. Above its doors the prominent white head of a roaring white lion stood out as its emblem for all to admire. What a sight it was. The White Lion Public House, its sigil always reminded me of a sabre-toothed tiger, let alone a roaring lion. Its fangs were prehistoric. As I got closer to the pub the music blared out of its smoky lamplight windows. The voices of its punters could be heard halfway across the main drag. I walked alone. I was my own man now. I footed the front steps of the pub.

"I.D", said the bouncer, bluntly. "Where is it?"

"I have it here," I replied.

"Give it to me now!" he exclaimed, and he placed a single hand in the middle of my chest to halt my progress. As I looked, his black Dicky bow was about to burst. He was a big beefy chap with no neck and a large round gut. Next to him was his right-hand man. He was just as tall, but wiry looking, with a weasely face. Their black and whites were a repellent to those that thought of starting any trouble. The guy that had stopped me was Head Bouncer without a doubt. Both had to be at least easily over thirty years old.

"There you go," I replied. I slipped him my driver's licence. It was legit. I wore blue stonewashed jeans, white shirt, smart leather Italian shoes, and had one big fuck off attitude.

He glared a long glare at me, as if he knew me, checking out my attire. He handed my license to his other counterpart but didn't break his glare from mine. *Weirdo*, I thought. Together they looked like a pair of uneducated soup waiters.

"In you go." He jeered.

Who was I to argue? In I went.

The bar was jammed. It was at least six deep. As I glare about, I spot those I am to rendezvous with. I grab my knock-on drink from the end of the bar then I go ahead and join them in the far top left corner. The sight was indeed jovial, happy faces. I got the odd card or two with the promise of a free drink next round, and a dance with a couple of the girls. If I played my cards right, who knows, I might be taking one home. I remember Madness playing on the neon-lit jukebox. Within moments we start to swap stories and catch up over long forgotten times. And boy, did time seem to fly. Before I knew it:

"Last orders!" called the Barmaid.

"It's my round," I said. "Let's have one more for the road." Why not? It wasn't often I spent time with my friends at home. I took my orders and sauntered off to the bar. As I walked the brass bell at the end of the bar was tolled. The town clock pinged in synchronisation with the bell. I squeeze next to an old lady smelling of lavender sat on a tall wooden stool. It was cold out. Ice was beginning to form on the windows, just as it did my old dormitory. *What a weird thought to have in a pub?* It's always amazed me how the mind works in times unseen. The old lady's brown fur coat seemed fluffed up, and was buttoned up to her chin. Out of politeness I offer to buy her a drink as I wait.

"Sherry, please," she replied, each of her fingers stacked with heaps of gold sovereign rings. The lipstick lined on her lips redder than that of the reddest poppy. Her smile reminded me of my mother.

There was a large growl at my rear. "Yer cunt!"

The chatting voices about me all stopped, but the jukebox kept playing. A drone of looming dread fell across the floor of the public house. I wonder what in the hell it was? A chill runs up my spine. I quickly turn to see. It was a man's voice. But not just any man's voice. It was the Head Bouncers voice.

"I said yer cunt!"

What's going on? I glare at the man as I turn. He squared up to me with his big chest, his gut much bigger. He was my height, but twice the weight, and had fat sausages for fingers. My gusts are doing summersaults right now. Then out of nowhere the other bounce appeared, smirking, chewing gum. Instantly, my breathing increased. The main bouncers face was screwed up like a bulldog licking piss of a nettle. Then, it suddenly turned red as beetroot.

"Do you need some medicine?" I joked. I thought it might lift his spirits. *Big mistake.* The old lady next to me burst out in fits of laughter. And come to think of it, so did the full pub, including my good self. "You look like you're in pain?" I said. "Would you like a paracetamol?" I reached into my jeans pocket. "I might have brought some with m —".

* CHAPTER 4*

~ The Division Bell ~

WHACK.

I fell to the floor like a sack of old potatoes. The hardness I was hit knocked my head backwards against the brass bell. Last orders had indeed tolled a second time. I knew I was down, but by golly I wasn't out.

"Fucker!" spat the Head Bouncer. His face was like a blown-up beetroot, the veins in his neck blistering.

"Cunt!" hollered the other.

The old lady fell off her stool in all the ruckus and landed face down on the brass foot bar. At least three pints of beer fell off the bar and spilled all over her red frock and fur coat. Her rings clang heavy against the metal as she attempts to break her own fall. The crack of gold on brass hurt my ears. *What the hell?* Instead, it was her face that struck the cast bar first.

Voices erupt in the public house. Those sympathetic to my cause, and that of the old lady screamed abuse at the bouncers in pleads of hatred and mercy.

"Get back! Get back!" the pair shouted, and they stuck out their chests and forced the crowds to one side.

The clock tower was on its third chime. I had eight to go. That's what my brain said to itself. Once the eight are done, your time is up. *Really? What then?*

"Back off!" The bouncers continued to chant at the crowds, and after a few seconds, all backed away, despite many being upset at the given situation. But that was the least of my worries.

"Grab him!" shouted one of them. "Get him now!"

They drag me into the foyer with my hair. As I look back the old lady is out cold. Her nose bloody, her eye cut. Then I smelt it again. It was just like before when I was four. Is that … *blood*? *It had been a while.* The beating of my heart increased in a flash. I could feel my eyes widen, my ears open, there was a pain inside my mouth, as if with pounding rage my teeth and my gums began to swell. *What the hell was going on with me?*

"Fucker!" they both cursed.

Instantly I reminisce of school - of Ivan Fray. My spatial awareness began to tingle. *Not again,* my brain says to me. *Please. Please, not again. I don't want any trouble. Not again.*

"*Going underground. Going underground.*" It was The Jam's turn to sing on the jukebox.

Both begin to lay the boot into me thick and hard as they dropped me near to the front doors. Steel toecap boots, black and shiny look quite pretty close up to your face, but all I could see was beauty, yet it didn't last long.

"Twat!" one cursed.

"Fucking cunt!" barked the other.

I curled up, my hands tight over my skull. Then I felt a solid foot drive a deep wedge into my bollocks. Each testicle, one by one, shot up like a bullet into my throat. My larynx grated against the flexible tenacity of my tonsils. The two black furtive shadows that stood over me reminded me of how vultures pick dead flesh from off a carcass. *I can't believe I was thinking of David Attenborough at a time like this?* Seething they lurched over me as the fluorescents burnt down into my eyes. *I can't see fuck all?* I remove my hands. *Now I asked for it.* The one with the big gut left a size eleven imprint on my cheek. I think my nostrils filled with some of my brains. *I think I've shit myself.* Then there was a punch at the base of my skull. *Or was it a kick?* I began to choke on my own blood. Then it was the ringing in my ears? *Was it tinnitus?* The room span out of control.

The town clock struck its tenth chime. It was nearly 11pm, just a second to go. People had gathered in the street, and apart from the jukebox, you could hear a pin drop outside. Then, quite bewildered, I felt a small flame growing inside me. In a flash, it rapidly grew into a huge fire, and then it blossomed into a roaring blast Furness. *Screw this.*

"You're going out yer cunt!" the Head Bouncer ordered. They reached down to grab me again but missed.

I rolled.

The last chime of the Town Clock struck as though the division bell was calling to my soul. I was up. "Don't take me!" I shout to the air and I look up into the night sky as if something – *abnormal* – was coming for me. I glared out and into the street, and up into the night sky above the Hill. But there was nothing, apart from white shiny dots glimmering faraway past the moon.

Both bouncer's seemed startled and looked also, but nothing was coming. Perhaps they thought it was an attempt to trick them. *Talk about thick or what,* I thought. Either way, it didn't go down too well. In fact, it made matters worse.

"Tosser!" the thin one spat.

"Get him!" growled the other.

I couldn't afford to fuck about. It was either kill or be killed. That was when I first realised that the smell of blood excited me. It gave me strength, and it was every-where. I wanted to lick it off the cold flagged floor as it swished about amidst dead cigarette butts. I had to have it in my mouth. All of it. My sight, my smell, all my senses became electrical; an eclectic feeling of sheer power drove over me. I felt alive. That was when I wanted to hurt them both – *badly*.

"Got you!" shouted the Head Doorman.

I didn't run. I didn't want to. Instead, I stood face to face with them both. So I edged them. Both were star-tled and let go. They stepped well back. The voices of those in the pub went quiet, and despite their pleas for mercy, people watched on. I took a deep breath and spat a wet glob-ule of bright red oxygenated blood down on to their shiny boots.

"Ops," I said. "It came up from my lungs. I felt it."

"Wipe it off now, or you'll get another beating," the big one ordered.

"It certainly couldn't be helped," I replied. "This is your fault." I spat again, but this time on the other door-man's shoe.

"Mother fucker!"

"Ops." I laughed, and so did those watching on. My body, already, was beginning to heal itself from inside; the beating of my heart slowed, my breaths became longer, the dark night became my ally. I reached up, and cracked my spine back into place, my two cracked ribs falling in asym-metrical line. I was ready now. I was ready now for war.

"Funny cunt!" says the thin one.

"Funny?" I repeated. "This isn't funny gentlemen. I'll tell you what's funny, shall I?"

The one with the big gut didn't flinch. I eyeballed them both. I listened, silently. There were whispers in the crowds behind me. I could hear both their chests a beat like a large drum. They were out of breath. I could hear their lungs wheezing, ever so slightly. I could smell them. It was a strange smell. I know that smell now to be *fear*.

"Now you're both going to die." *Let's see what response I get,* I thought. I said it softly. Almost a whisper. The last I wanted was to startle them – *not*.

"Eh?" said the thin bouncer, as if startled, but desperate not to show it.

"Did I not say it loud enough gentlemen?" I replied. Now I was going to toy with them. So again, I repeat it ever so calmly. I whispered it ever so faintly. "Now you both die …"

They both gulped. "Really?" they replied.

"Are you ready, gentleman?" I brushed myself down. Out of my pocket I take my handkerchief, its initials embroidered into its corner. I dab at the blood on my lips. I then suck my handkerchief, and my eyes roll into the back of my skull at the sheer thrill of the taste. "Delicious," I remark.

"What the fuck are you doing?" said the big one.

"Have you ever tasted your own blood?" They both seemed a little wary. "It tastes so lush." I laugh a little at my antics. I set my eyes upon them, then I stepped closer. *Was taunting them the right thing to do?* It felt normal, though, like a cat playing with a dead mouse. God it felt good. There was dust on my white shirt from the foyer floor, and a boot print on my stomach, and bright red blood down my front. I peered hard at the pair, but not looking at them directly, but through them in jest. I smiled, and showed my teeth, only slightly. These guys were a problem, a disease in fact, and with problems, it's always good to see past the problem to the end result: the solution. And in my mind, I had already defeated them.

"You're going to kill us both?" They laughed hard, except I heard it. I heard both their heartbeats go up a notch. Then there was that smell again, even worse than before: *fear.* The Head Bouncer stepped forward in his attempt to illustrate his authority, except, I saw right through it. Lest we forget, this guy was on show in front of the full public house, as well as those out in the street. He didn't want to feel de-masculinised, but the guy had a problem - neither did I.

The black hair on my head resembled that of a bog brush. Like piss-holes in the snow my eyes of blue watered with bloodshot red. Then Nigel Benn *The Dark Destroyer* and his fight with Ian Chantler fleeted my vision. Benn knocked him out in 16 seconds. *Was it my spiritual being talking to me? Was I getting instruction on how to survive this attack?*

"CUNT!" The Head Bouncer barked, though I stood my ground and smiled most appeased.

"I've been know of better names," I jest.

"TWAT!" shouted the other.

"That wasn't what I had in mind," I laugh, and i smile to taunt the big fucker. I even put both my hands in my pockets in a display of fearlessness – or perhaps an action of stupidity, or complete arrogance in their opinion. *Did I care?* This, in all, was a feigning tactic to get them to attack – much like the tactics used by the Weaver Spider. I wanted to seem to them to be vulnerable because it worked a treat. Talk about reverse psychology. As soon as I did, like a bullet at my skull, he shot at me, his big sausage-finger fists flying.

"Ops," I said. I darted to his left. I let rip.

"Bastard", he hissed.

SMACK.

The Head Bouncer fell to the ground in a pile of blubber. I turned sharply on one foot and fronted the other. His chin dropped in awe.

"Now your turn." I edged him, just like before.

"I don't want any trouble," he fretted instantly, and as he shifted back he fell backwards over the fat one onto the stone flags. I stood over him, menacingly, fists still clenched like rocks.

"Help!" he cried, though all in the pub and out on the streets laughed. "Don't hurt me", he cried. "Mercy! Mercy!"

"You're not laughing now?" I was ripping with rage.

The crowds began to clap loudly. He covered his head expecting me to kick him, but instead, I turned and walk back to the main foyer. The anger I had harboured for years against Ivan Vray had come back to visit me. It was as though a dark shadow knocked upon my door to get in. I used it to my advantage, as I do today, and do every day after that. That feeling of rage consumed me irrevocably. It engulfed my senses as though it the Grim Reaper come to collect recompense on my soul. But there was something else. For the first time ever I felt the hunger for human flesh.

How tasty it looks, I whispered to myself. I knelt down in front of the big bouncer out cold. I poked him with one finger on his cheek. I wanted to take a bite out of his face. Just one. *Would it hurt?* I wanted to taste sweet cheeks. The flesh looked so plump and tasty and pink. I licked my own red lips as I taste my own blood. *One bite wouldn't hurt, would it?* Then I heard voices near. I turned sharply. I was being watched. For a moment I had zoned out. The music of the jukebox began to play once more.

Going underground. Going underground …

A dark silence in my dark mind festered. Though it sounds odd, I wanted to be attacked again. I wanted to feel provoked. I wanted to feel that power to want to kill.

"Victor!"

"Yes?" I turn. It was the old lady.

"Help an old lady to her feet, would you?" In her best efforts to rise, she had hurt her arm, and her face was swollen badly. As I got there others were already helping her to her feet. I picked her up and sat her back down on the stool at the end of the bar.

"Thank you my dear."

"Watch that bell from now on", I chuckled. "I can only apologise for what happened."

"You have done so well," she said. "I've been watching. This was not your doing. This was the doing of men, greedy men, hegemonic men, patriarchal men, uncaring men; men unfit to be in a position of trust and rule and power." Off her stool she hopped and strode over to the big doorman. She stood over him, then kicked him on his leg. "Arsehole!" There were many that laughed at the site of it.

"Do you feel better now?" I asked.

"That felt good. He was a bully," she said. "Nasty, horrible man. All bullies get their comeuppance in the end."

That was odd? I thought. Then it hit me. *How did she know my name? Perhaps I told her, or did I?*

People in the street cheered, claps echoed throughout the Town Square. I stepped over both bouncers and walked out and down the stone steps of the pub and into the street. *Boy did I feel good.* The old lady knocked on the window and waved at me from the inside the pub. There she raised a toast in my absence with her sherry.

Inside my head I began to plan my route home. I didn't even feel the cold, but a new feeling took me. *Was that his voice I could hear?* I focused in harder. *It can't be, surely?* I stop and turn. I could hear the bees nesting all the way up in the clock tower, the birds sleeping in the trees of the nearby church, the rain a hail on the top of Pendle Hill adjacent to the Nick 'O' Pendle – a storm of sorts was brewing. *What the hell?* I glare hard into the darkness of the crowds. *Was it actually him?* I tore through people to get a better look. I didn't even have to think about it. Yes it was dark, but still. The people near to me parted like the Red Sea. *Is it him?* I looked harder. Then I see him. I smell him.

"Impossible," I say aloud.

He was stood tall, his back resting below the glow of an orange streetlamp. The black baseball cap he had on covered his eyes. As I neared, he peered out from the far back of the crowds, his lackeys nearby. *I like it. I like it a lot.* At the last second, he sees me glaring right at him. The game is up. *It was Ivan Vray. I have you now.* I point at the man in the baseball cap.

"YOU!" I hollered.

Startled, the guy flits his eyes about him to see if I'm pointing at anyone else. He soon figures I'm not. "M-me?" he says.

"Yes! *You?*"

Those that know me see me see him. Whispers of jeer begin to beckon in the cold night. In an instant his lackeys scarper off into the darkness as though roaches away from daylight. *What cowards.* Many people about him disband. I approach swiftly. The smell of autumn leaves drift overhead from wind-bearing trees off the town park. The street was cobbled, but my path was led. The rain in the air was getting closer. The damp of autumn had at last come.

"Do *NOT* move," I holler.

The man stumbles back over the kerb as I near. He falls with his back against the Swan Public House wall. It *was* him. I'd taken him by complete surprise. I see he's nervous, his heart beat like a drum. I had my finger adamantly pointing right at him, my spirit ever-looming. I bite down hard on my teeth. I front him, face to face. His eyes are at my level, wide, his pupil's dilated. I wanted this man to see me. To see me hard.

"If it isn't good old Mr. Vray," I announce to my onlookers. I was taller, my chest and back much wider, my voice deeper. All fear at last had left me like the dusty sands from over the Sahara.

"Victor," he replied, with penitence in his voice. His breathing quickened. I stand and wait.

"…and?"

For the first time he looks *at* me like I once did him: *frightened.* "I'm waiting," I said. He broke his gaze. "Look me in the eye, Ivan," I barked, but he cowered like a dog. He gulped hard. I felt his fear.

"But-"

I taunt him. "Coward."

"Well … erm … but …"

Like iron rods my fists became clenched. I remembered my pain, and the embarrassment. The dinner queues. The flying spaghetti. How those that called themselves my friends abandoned me. I was now in the zone. A small fleet of Goosebumps skims my skin. I remember the anxiety that he caused. I'm readying myself to smack him right in the mouth at any moment. I'm revved up like a racehorse.

Now I hated spaghetti hoops from a tin. The once suicidal thoughts flash in my vision. His face, his face once haunted the silence of my days and my never-ending nights.

"Victor," he went on, but hesitated in mid flow.

The skies opened as thick rain cascade down upon the hilly streets. The cobbles shone like slimy pebbles on a beach at high tide. I wanted to hurt this man, badly. I moved closer to him. I wanted to bite his face. *What the fuck was I thinking? Shall I lick his cheeks instead? I put both hands in my pockets. Let's see if the fucker tries it on.*

"Well?"

"I don't want any trouble, V-victor." He fretted. His voice was timid. *Where were his lackeys now?* They were nowhere in sight.

"But I was never given that choice, was I, Ivan? What makes you believe that I will honour your request? Do you take me for a fool?"

"I saw what you did to those bouncers." Ivan stayed staunch, but his eyes were down to the ground. "You knocked the fat one out. I've never seen anyone do that to him before. He's a grown man. At least in his mid-thirties. You're only nineteen."

I whip both hands out my pockets. I make a hard fist. Ivan jumped and raised his arms up to his head as if to protect his face. I'll uppercut the fucker. He won't even see it coming. I was a nanosecond away, then he said something that I did not expect.

"Forgive me. *Please.* Won't you forgive me, Victor?" There was tremble within his voice.

I blink a few times. "W-what?"

The wind is howling, the crowds unmoving, and the rain is pelting off my bare skin. Steam begins to rise from my body. Ivan also is pissed wet through.

"My father beats me," he admitted. "Even now he beats me, Victor." A tear of shame came to the corner of his eye. He sobbed uncontrollably. "I am s-sorry." He put his head down in shame.

I was taken aback. Literally. I stepped back, stumbled more like out of complete shock. *What the hell,* I whisper. He'd totally knocked the wind out of my sails. *Did he just say what I thought he did?* The crowds tsked and mumble with sordid contempt. At first, I didn't know what to make of it. *Is he telling the truth? Is he genuine?* I glared hard. I glared long. He did not look me in the eye. He was vigorously shaking. People near to me chant the words of long, sweet revenge. I hear some in the crowds telling others how this guy had bullied me for years. That he was going to get what he deserved. That it was long time coming for, Ivan. Then aside from wanting to hurt him, my focus eventually became affixed on one thing: *I am better than this man.*

"I am not the man you think I am, Victor," Ivan blurted. "I am not that bully anymore."

"No shit!" I was furious. But at that moment I realised that I was now Ivan, and Ivan was now me. The acknowledgement of his fear became apparent to me like the tiny silver droplets of morning dew strewn freely upon a sunlight patch of wet meadow. The once ponderous chains of being bullied that hung weighted upon my neck were now cracked and torn, a sincere feeling of self-gratification shod over my bearing. I was done with this man. This chapter in my life was now complete. From here on, I could move on. This guy was a dead beat, and that's all he'll ever be – a leach living off the fear of others.

"Please, Victor," Ivan went on.

I took a deep sigh, then relished in the thought of reimbursement of emotional rift; not my rift, but his. I stepped up close to Ivan's face. I was but an inch from his nose. *Shall I lick his face?* "Take this as a warning, Ivan."

"I will, Victor. I will. Thank you. *Thank you.*" He sobbed. "I felt forced to do what I did. Forgive me, please, Victor. I knew not any better."

Felt forced? I had the man beat. I turned away from him slowly, then I gave him a glare of farewell, though still, his head was low. I walked away, those on the street now heading off in various directions. The show was over. For some, the night was still young. I head back down the street; a flash of distant lightning over Pendle Hill strikes the black air. I take a look up at the White Lion as I make my way home, the old lady still waving, her sherry with ice in hand. I walked bare chested that night. I had no choice, though, in all, my mood methodical, a settled anger seethed through my veins. *Maybe I should've given the guy a slap? Did he deserve it?* I will never cower again in my life to *any* man. As I walk, I contemplate over the night's events. The further I walk, the more my mood begins to simmer. Though it was bleak, winter was here, and any snow that landed upon my back melted. Maybe I was that angry that I was numb to my environment. It was a long walk, but nevertheless, overall, it was well needed.

As I hit the long gravel path to my home, I could hear the bats whizzing past my head, flicking my hair; the foxes rummaging in the bracken hunting rabbits; Billy Brock snooting in the earth just fields away in search for its favourite food: leatherjackets. *Perhaps I was losing it?* I take a turn in the path and there I catch a glimpse of the distant porchlight. It was so inviting to me. I remember feeling that a new chapter was about to come, that I would tell my father of my triumphs, and he will share upon the joys of my victories.

That, unfortunately, was not the case.

I reach the threshold of my home; the bright moon bore down upon me, the gravel underfoot crunches as I near. I unlock the front door with my key.

* CHAPTER 5*

~ Breakfast in a Heartbeat ~

"Where *have* you been?"

The voice startled me. I'm caught off guard. "Pardon?" I whispered.

"What time do you call this?" My mother's face had turned sour. "Shirt ripped? Who do you think you are – Tarzan?"

"I didn't mean to wake anyone."

The Grandfather clock in the hallway chimed midnight with a low cursing bell as the latch to the front door is locked and bolted. I turn to face the music.

"I was awake." She threw a towel at me disgruntled. "Now dry off. Quick about it."

I take it without comment or thought. She pulls me up a chair in the kitchen. "Now sit."

"O.K".

"Keep still." Out of her dressing gown pocket she pulls this small bottle of yellow liquid with a handful of cotton wool buds. "This is going to hurt."

I get comfy, the towel over my shoulders. *Why was she carrying that in her pocket at this time?* The atmosphere turns to rhetorical tension through torture with yellow medicine.

"You have cuts all over your face. Your ribs are bruised, too."

"I got in a fi-..."

"I do not want to know. We will talk in the morning."

I am reminded by God of how insignificant I truly am. *That hurt more than a smack in the mouth. Who the fuck invented this shit?* It throbbed like hell hath no fury. As I focused in it looked just like a bottle of cat piss, but smelt far worse. It wasn't the pain in my face from my beating that kept me awake that night. It was the pissy smell of TCP all over my head and lips. The next thing I hear is the call from my mother.

"Breakfast is up!"

It was daybreak, though it was still dark outside. I quickly brush my teeth, throw on my slacks and head downstairs. My father can't stop staring at my face. In my mind I must've looked much like a pumped up black and blue bruised turnip. But before I'm questioned, I tell him of my victory at the pub and of Ivan Fray, though I do not boast. *Well, he did look as if he wanted to know.*

"I see," his reply solemn.

Was he not pleased? I thought.

"Your mother last night said your face was bruised and swollen." He reached forward and picked up a piece of toast.

"Do I look a mess?"

"Except now there is nothing? Not a mark in sight." The expression on his face didn't change. I knew he was being serious. A man of his position always was.

"Pardon?" I reply. *Was he taunting me?*

He shrugged, pacifyingly, then nodded towards the hallway door.

I fly to the mirror out in the hall. I glare ravenously. There was not a scar, or a bruise in sight. *What the hell? Is that TCP magical?* I must've missed that when I brushed my teeth. I march back to the kitchen, a cloud of unsurity looming over my sanity. *Was I losing it?* "That's impossible,"

I remarked. I pulled up a chair and sat down. *Did I dream it?*

"Perhaps your beating wasn't that bad?" He said, jesting almost, yet he wasn't.

Was he messing with me? I didn't retaliate verbally, though he sat a while and sipped his tea. He pondered deep, his expression burdened. I could sense it. Not once did he take his eyes from mine. In the end I had to look away. Ida was preparing a full English breakfast and was about to serve up. The many pots and pans clinked on the stove. My father took a small bite of his toast with another slurp of his hot tea to swill it down.

"I have waited for a day like this to come for a long time." Robert glared harder.

"Really?" *What was he trying to say? I had never got into a fight in my whole life. I hated violence of any kind.*

"Be easy on him, Robert," Ida was my shield, though they had over the years played *'Good Cop: Bad Cop.'* My father was good at that.

"Mother saw how bad the injuries I sustained last night. Didn't you mother?" I gave her a glance, but she was busy with breakfast, the crackle of the bacon and eggs sizzling drowning out my voice … either that or she didn't want to get involved in the politics of parenting. I went to bed with a broken head, and now I wake up like Jack and fucking Jill. Except, no brown paper or vinegar was there to mend my 'bloody' head. It seemed to have fixed itself all on its own during the night. *Perhaps God came down and healed me while I was sleeping?* My father didn't take well to the lord's name being used in blasphemy. I best keep my mouth tight shut on that theory.

"There is only one race – the human race," my father stated. "We are all innocent in the eyes of God, but not in the eyes of our fellow man."

"What *is* going on?" I said. *What the hell was all that about?* I sit still, then I begin to feel a little edgy. It was his eyes. His eyes met mine with a look I had never seen before. The pump in my chest goes up a notch, the pupils in my eyes dilate to the size of two silver dollars. His glare, though ominous, brought me to my senses. *Did this guy want to fight me?* Surely not? He was my father. I anticipate with scepticism in such a way that I begin to shuffle in my chair. *I think I'm paranoid.* My head and my senses were all over the place as if like an off-kilter compass. *What was he thinking?*

"Well?" He went on as if he knew what I was to say about it all? He lifted his tea to his mouth. "I'm waiting." *Slurp. Slurp.*

"Well, what?" In a way, I felt grown up, with a sense of pride and belong, that I had resolved a long, way-overdue lingering 'mental' problem. I had evicted my unpaying tenant. *Didn't all bullies someday get their comeuppance? If so, they fucking both did.*

"Freedom of mind is priceless to those in barter for their lives."

There he goes again. What the hell? "I don't understand, father," I replied. This, no doubt, was another one of his many hidden-meaning-talks again. For years he had taunted me with the riddles of the world, the losses of the few, the deaths of the unseen, and for what?

"We can rationalise that all things in life happen for a reason, Victor," He took another bite of his toast – a slow bite - and another hearty sip. He finished chewing first; I hated when he did that. Always keeping me in suspense, as though an unruly delinquent sat on a chair of persecution, letting me hang on his every word. "Never go looking for trouble, and hope that trouble never comes looking for you."

"Ivan was a bully." Let's face facts, he was. "He made my life a living hell. The last year at school was horrific. He flung spag…"

"Only when you attended school, Victor. I know of your truancy. I know of you self-isolating at home hiding in the loft away from your troubles rather than confronting them, studying alone. You have your mother's good fortune of heart to thank for that. If I had my way, you'd've been at school every day, until your very last day."

I go quiet; the floppy white things on the sides of my face called cheeks tighten and go bright red. I then gulped. I even heard my Adams apple go down hard all the way to hell. This is where the guy gives me a clout behind my ear for the first time in history. I get ready for the crack.

"But alas … not to worry." He smiled. He takes a sigh of relief, but not his relief, it was mine. "All that is in the past now." He smiled again. He was appeasing me, as if to say, *I've got one up on you. I know something you don't. What chores was he to have me do now?* "You're a man now, Victor. Now you're nineteen." He smiled yet a third time, though loosely. *What did he mean by that? Yes, he could complete the Guardian newspaper crossword in less than five minutes, but was this some sort of a cryptic clue?*

"Place it to the back of your mind, son." He looked at me stern. "All things happen for a reason, right?"

The guy knew I'd been playing truant most of the year and didn't confront me about it? Why on earth not? *Who had the fuck told him?* I guess now wasn't the time to ask. Let's face it, the world is a cruel place, and the people that run it are even cruller. I didn't want to get on my father's bad side. Not that he'd ever beaten me, let alone put me over his knee growing up. I just had a lot of respect for the guy, and for mother too. But he was right. I did play truant, but at least at that time it took me away from any potential confrontation with Ivan. I wanted to feel 'anxiety free' for once in my life. I wanted to hold my head up high and not be seen as a coward. That wasn't much to ask, was it for a boy of sixteen? It was the last I needed at that time. *But why didn't he ever pull me up on it previously?*

"Your mother told me this morning of your escapades last night out in the Town Square. I am surprised you weren't arrested. I can only assume the police were out catching proper criminals, not having to deal with petty fist fights in a drunken brawl (*...drunken brawl? How dare he say that. I was attacked!* I thought.) Then I am told your face was beaten beyond recognition. That you may have had a cracked rib or two? ..."

Hold on? I didn't tell my mother anything about what happened in Clitheroe Town last night or what injuries I had sustained due to feeling the cold steel of toe cap boots drive up into my groin.

"...If I am correct in my medical diagnosis: the 7th and 8th left cage; a ruptured spleen, a cracked medial phalanx of the third digit of your right hand; a left mild cranial fracture; a fractured left cheek bone, along with a rupture to your left aspect temporomandibular joint. Then on top of that, a central retinal vein occlusion to your left eye, and a ruptured left testicle. Yet, this morning you have awoken as if nothing has happened. You are today - *unscathed.*" He said all this rather quickly as if on handover from one doctor to another at the local hospital. *I had watched E.R once or twice. What the heck?*

"Lastly, a left bicipital tear, and left pneumothorax." *What the hell did he just say? What medical jargon bullshit was that?* I was stunned. I'd never heard him talk like this before. Not once. I was numb. I blinked a few times, not sure how many, but I must've looked totally stupid.

"But ho-"

"Drink you coffee son." He said.

I didn't want coffee right now. I had to say something. "I didn't tell my mother about my ribs. The last I wanted was for her to worry. They felt sore, that's all. By the time I got home, they were, well, better. The long walk and fresh air must've helped."

"I see," he said. Up he stood. Had I done something wrong? *Was he going to give me a crack, nonetheless?* "Come with me." He set off on foot, his slippers backless, and he tightened his dressing gown belt.

"O.K."

"Back in a jiffy." He said to Ida.

"Breakfast will be ready in two minutes boys. I don't want it going cold," she said factly.

Robert whisked me into the hall where he stood me flat faced in front of the mirror. His crucifix on a gold chain tucked beneath his dressing gown was popping out. Subtly, he placed his arm around my shoulder. We stood side by side, eye to eye, his head easily the same height as my own. His beard was now greying, his head piebald with flecks of silver hair. He had a stern reflection, his features mature and masculine and young for his age, his jawline solid, his eyes piercingly bright and light blue.

I had to ask. "What exactly are we doing, father?"

He shrugged his shoulders. He took another bite of his toast as if a cow gently chewing its cud. Then a bolt of images hit me in my head. *Was I dreaming? I saw it clearly, like the rising sun from the east of the land. There were a flash in my eyes of my father running naked in the Forest of Pendle, the moon high in the night sky, his thick silhouette full and fast upon the horizon. He was in chase of a mighty black bear.*

"Your face is unscathed," he stated. "Why do you think that is?" he glared on in silence. Then, in goes the toast again. *Hadn't he eaten the darn thing yet?* He was beginning to irritate me with his slow ways.

"What?" I was in a daze. "How do you mean?" but he didn't reply. I could smell the bacon, hear the eggs sizzling in the pan. I got my focus back quickly. "I'm n-not sure what you mean, father?"

"Think about it. Think about it *very* (very) carefully. Close your eyes and think – *deep.*"

I nodded, so as asked i closed my lids. The bacon was sizzling. It smelt so good. We stood a while, me listening, smelling. I open my eyes. He raised his eyebrows, as if in gloat. *What was he doing? I knew what he was doing – he was trying to piss me off.*

"Are we there yet, Victor?" He bit his toast, and began to chew again. Bloody Nora.

I noticed something. I felt it coming. It was glaring straight at me ... something *eerie.* I felt my senses switch on again, just like last night when I was attacked when cornered. There was a sense of déjà vu about me. *This wasn't happening right now, was it?* I focused in tight. Then as though a brick in my teeth – *bang.* A sense of retrouvaille swilled through every orifice of my soul. I was falling. I was falling fast and hard. I couldn't contain myself. I began to breathe quickly, my adrenaline pumped hard, the cold liquid coursed my veins. It was my eyes; they became sharp and light, and my gums again began to swell ...

"Well?" He said lastly. "Are we there yet?"

"You're dead!" There was no heartbeat in my father's chest.

"That I am, lad." His eyes flashed over, as if his body was going into hunt mode. I sensed it inertly. His face changed. He became fierce; like that night he caught up with the black bear and ripped out its throat.

I set off at speed.

"Why do you run, son?"

I sprint further down the hallway, sort of sideways away from him at first, my feet fumbling on the first step to the stairs. I cracked my skull on the bannister. I zoned out again, then in. I was on it. *How the fuck do I get out? I'd only lived here for the last fifteen years but where the fuck is the front door?*

"Shall we fight, Victor?"

"Stop teasing him," said Ida. "Breakfast is nearly out, boys."

I knew it. "Mother is dead, too?" I holler. The pair of them both dead as fuck.

"That she is. You've no need to flee." Robert held up his hands as if innocent, probably hoping I'd not flee. Except it didn't work. *Would you hang about with weirdos like this? I mean, what the fuck were these people?*

"Stop! Victor?" He shouted.

I flew up the flight of stairs as if a gazelle, four steps at a time, then tripped at the top. I try and correct my leap but fall on the landing just off the top step. I had skin burns on my face from the carpet. Then I was up. I glimpsed back. *Where is father? Where has he gone?*

"Keep calm, Victor." I turn to see. The guy was stood behind me. He bit down on his toast again, the loud crunch of the burnt bread in my ears. *Freak!*

"Help me!" I cried, but to whom, I had no idea.

"I *am* here to help." He said. "We both are, Victor."

From the landing I jump and land hard at the bottom. I rolled on the floor. I'm up. I fly for the front door. I open it, latch and all. I didn't look back. I run out into the frosty light. *What the hell?* I run less than ten feet then land square upon my back on the snowy path. He was in front of me. I bounced off his chest as if he's a rock of solid iron. Dazed I glare about. The guy has his slippers on for Christ's sake. It wasn't as if he was wearing a pair of Adidas trainers, or part of Aladdin's flying carpet stitched to the rear of his heels. This guy could burn some rubber. I didn't even see him come past me? I'm up. I set off again.

"Victor, please?" He set off after me trailing at my rear. *Is he taunting me?*

I reach the gate at the end of the winding path that heads out through the perimeter wall. Trees overshadow my rear, large rhododendron bushes, leafless, hydrangeas loom nearby. I turn. There is a damp smell of rotting leaves and black earth in the wind. Then I saw him, there, in the shadows he is stood again, chewing his ruddy toast, slurping his tea. *What the fuck was going on?* Now he had a cup of tea in his hand?

"What are you man?" I shout.

"I am your father, Victor."

"You are dead, dude!"

"You call me dead, yet you are the one who can hear a person's heartbeat from a hundred yards? That you have the ability to smell another man's blood? The ability to think (and see) into another man's soul."

"Listen to your father, Victor."

Freaking hell? There in the grey winds, pine trees amidst her backdrop were stood my mother. "I do not want my breakfast going cold. I've been up since the crack of dawn cooking. Do you think it fair for good food to be wasted? Now come back in the house and let's eat, son."

"I've lost my appetite!" There she stood, kitchen baggin wrapped around her waist, hair net on, frying pan in hand; eggs and bacon still sizzling, blistering hot, bubbling against the snowy wet weather. I watched as snowflakes land on my bacon, for the bacon fat to spit into my eye. *Ouch!* Barefoot, slushy snow popping out between her toes she disappears back into the house at a lightning speed. There one second, gone the next. "Come back into the house, Victor!" Mother shouted from the kitchen window. I blinked and rubbed my eyes.

"Let us eat, Victor. We can talk about this around a hearty table. We can light the hearth and talk in the warmth and comfort of our home," said father. "Won't you come back indoors, son?"

"What the hell are you people?" I was long gone.

They were insane. I had to escape this asylum. I am in the Dark Wood. The premise was simple. I had no choice. I darted off deep into the forest, zigging and zagging as if escaping a crocodile. The sun was not yet up. It was pitch black, the moon nesting down behind the far west horizon. I run for what feels like an age, ducking and diving, cuts across my face from whipping branches. I hid tight against a wide tree. I slumped down amidst its thick roots at the helm of the wet forest floor. I drag autumn leaves about me and take rest amongst a set of up-poking roots. I throw over more dead leaves. I had to rest. This was a head fuck, a proper head fuck. I took deep breaths and wiped my brow. *What the fuck just happened?* I stay completely still, my warm breath rising in silver mist to the dark air. But it didn't last long. It wasn't long before he was on me.

"Late last night just before you arrived home, we received a phone call from Edna Calvesfoot."

"Edna who?" I shout, though I keep well hidden. I

appease the guy, taking time to think what to do next.

"Edna is the lady in the pub you so kindly purchased a sherry for. You're not a boy anymore. I lied to you Victor." He said all this with toast in his mouth, tea dribbling down his lips as he stood proudly in his slippers and dressing gown in the forest. I look up, but he's gone. *Where the hell are you man?* There is a rustling of trees, a crack of branches, the fall of lose bark drops onto me from above. I shield my eyes as the sun breaks from over the Hill as I glare upwards into the forest canopy. He was above me in the fucking trees jumping from bow to bow, branch to branch. Dark shadows flitted over me in the awakening wood.

Outstanding? I thought. *Even the old dears were now spying on me. Didn't Edna-whats-her-face have anything else better to do?* I decide to shout out. "What was I supposed to do, father? Always you told me stories of Bare-knuckle Bob. He was your father, was he not?" I make myself heard. "Was that not who HE was? I was attacked by two grown men. They got what they deserved. An eye for an eye. A tooth for a tooth, right?"

"Do not use the lord's name in blasphemy. I carry *His* sigil upon me."

I couldn't see my father anywhere. *Was it safe to go? Sack this shit.* I set off again, sprinting. *Shall I head to the train station and go back North to Bonnie Scotland?*

"I am with you," he shouted. "I always have been, son."

Soon I come to the cliff face at Witches Quarry. A long stony drop appeared as if out the thicket of trees. The ledge was upon me. It was barely daylight, and I was cornered, not unless I turn back. *Not on your Aunt Nelly*. A huge open space is before me, a deep, dark green watery tarn below.

"And look where Bob is now? He's either been killed, or kidnapped. Nobody knows? His body has never been found. But deep down I know my brother is still alive. Do you not feel it, Victor?"

"You are barking, man!" I detest. "You and your wife are a pair of freaks""

Search your soul. Look for his memories in me, only then will you see him for yourself."

"Listen to your father, Victor."

Jesus Christ! I freak out. "I'm not hungry, mother." And then there was that sound? The sizzle of bacon and sausages and the aroma of baked beans, mushrooms and tomatoes cooked deliciously on the stove as the aroma of it idled through the wet dense woodland trees. I could smell it. *How was that possible?* I was all the way through the woods, at least a mile away. But guess what? Here she is, three pans in her arms, one scalding her forearms as she held out the other two. She glares at me then smiles.

"Would you like to taste these beans?"

"What?"

"They're your favourite, Victor. Here. Try a spoon-ful." Out she held a spoon with a mound of beans on it, piping hot. *You're dead dude!*

"Scrummy, scrummy says mummy."

I refused bluntly. Then off she shot again, the kitchen door slamming as she entered the house, the smashing of a cup or glass on the floor, probably by her mistake. I heard it hit the tiled floor. I curl up tight and hide behind a bush. I can see the quarry's edge. *Shall I jump and hope for the best? Its only water at its base? I've done it as a kid before? Then I'm home free.* I take a deep breath. Fuck it, why not. *Yes, let's do it!*

"We don't want that for you," shot my father's voice

from out of the distant trees.

The forest was overcast with broken specs of light, parts of it greying as daylight struck its huge sprawled out, bough's.

I was still bordering on jumping. *Shall I jump?* Suddenly, there was a noise. *Wasn't there?* The trees rustled in the high winds, the leaves a stir about me, my vision distorted. There it was again, a cracking noise? Perhaps he is near. *Was he?* I look all about me. The wood had gone darker, as if the trees had closed in around me, their thin branches stroking the top of my head like long fingers reaching to grab me, keeping me against my will. *Do it now.* I had to jump.

"You're our son, Victor."

"Then who the hell are you?"

"If you bring trouble to this door, or place your troubles upon others, then it affects all of us. Not just you. We must keep our secret safe. We must keep our world, safe."

"Our secret? Our world?" *What the hell does he mean? Our secret? Our world? What allegory bullshit was this?*

"Trust in me, Victor."

I shuffle closer to the edge to look over. *Trust?* The snow was crunchy underfoot. One move and I would slip. Over the tarn there was a clearing of trees, and the dim light of the sky shone down as a deep grey blizzard came out the blue. Icy winds with drifting snow from over Pendle Hill had come. From the corner of my eye I could see the remote peak of it beneath a haze of looming mist. I glared harder, I could see the people upon its peak, marching through the snowy meadows as if I had the eyes of a hawk. I rubbed my eyes hard. *I must've hit my head a little funny.*

"Come home, son!"

"Leave me be!" I shouted. But it was too late. He

was upon me. It was just me and him now. He approached me tenderly through the thickets of pines and held out his hand to pull me back. I did not take it. I turned to face him more. Then the moment took me without consent. I sank to my knees in the mud. I think I am going into shock. This was not happening right now. I simply could *not* believe this was true.

Deep breaths, think Victor, stay calm. You are flying now. You are doing this alone. Take flight my child. Soar on the winds sent to you from the Hill.

"But I will fall," I said to the voice.

"You are of our bloodline. A bloodline we thought once extinct, until the finding of your blood." Robert made a grab for me, fast and hard.

I slipped. The green of the tarn was coming for me.

* CHAPTER 6*

~ Deliver Us From Evil ~

Rat-a-tat-tat.

I awoke with a start. It was the front door. I could feel the drool running down my lips as if I'd be seriously smacked in my mush. My head was throbbing like the core of a drum. *Where in hell?* I was sat back in the kitchen chair. *What the hell?*

"Breakfast is up," said mother. She began to serve up.

For a moment I felt flabbergasted. The smell of bacon and eggs and beans lifted my senses. I was so hungry. *But why? Had I fallen asleep at the kitchen table? Had I been dreaming again?*

"Fall asleep did you, Victor?" The guy was still sat there eating his freaking toast, a hot steaming mug of tea in hand. Always has he said that drinking tea relaxed him, and helped him think?

"Serve up the breakfast to Ivan first Ida dear. He's a growing lad."

I was not wet? *Had I not fallen into the tarn?* My attire was as clean as a silver button, still in my black slacks and white t-shirt, even my trainers were dry, too. *How odd?*

"Look sharp." Politely, humbly, Ida shifted around the kitchen filling up our plates. Tea was poured, toast was buttered, hot coffee was on the stove on a light heated-plate simmer. I lifted my top, as if in a haze. I had no injuries to my body, either.

"The police are here. I heard them driving up the

avenue. I heard the gate go. You have brought them here to this house. This is *your* doing." He fixated his vision on me. Off he set to the door.

"Hold on a second," I said to my mother. "What just happened before? What does he mean the police are here?" Her feet were pissed wet through with iced water, twigs and bracken popping out of her toes. Then I smelt it. Her toe was cut, her oxygenated red blood mixed white with bright white snow. Not only that, even above the aroma of the breakfast, I could smell it. It smelt so dam good. Within a flash my eyes flocked towards her feet. They looked tasty all of a sudden. *What was I thinking? Meaty toes? Seriously? I needed to give my head one hell of a shake.*

Her face did not falter. "I've seen that look before, Victor. It won't do you any good. Trust me. I've killed bigger men for less."

"Wh-.."

"Listen carefully before your father returns." She stood still with the pan in her hands, sizzling with fried eggs, just like in the forest. Her eyes bore into me. "You are the lost bloodline of Sir. William Wallace. You have his heritage. You have now come of age. And you are immortal, and if you drink the blood of another immortal, you will die."

Was the lady shitting me? Who the fuck was she? What does she mean, killed bigger men? "I don't understand?"

"All will make sense eventually, Victor." She smiled and carried on, as if for her she was simply talking about the antics of the weather over the telephone. Except little did I realise, bad weather was about to come. "You're a man now, Victor. Life for you *will* change forever."

I was in a haze, glaring into nothingness. *What the hell did she just say?* Ida used the kitchen tea towel to quickly mop up the blood, muttering indignantly about how she was clumsy with the glass. Then on went her slippers with a wrap of kitchen role about her big toe. But it was still bleeding. I could smell it.

"Now I've got the glass out it'll heal in no time."

Mother always spoke to herself. It was her niche.

"Victor?"

"Yes". I sifted my eyes towards the doorway to the hall. It was my father. With him two tall men stood by his side, each with blue peaked caps emblazoned with a seven-pointed Silver Star.

"These police officers would like a word, Victor. Ida, best serve up some tea for these strapping lads." Ida always loved visitors, for often she would play the perfect host.

I stood and shook both their hands firmly. I invited them to sit at our table, surrendering my seat. My father gave me a look of distasteful indignation. It was a look that reflected do tell the truth, but don't indulge into other telling's. It was fine. I got the message.

That day my spirit sank, literally down to the very bottom of my toes. I realised then that the long sense of jubilation over my recent triumphs was now gone. I could never relive the telling of my tale of victory. A silent death lingered. The Ferryman had come for me, except I didn't have his payment in silver for him to take me across the raging rapids. Now I was up shit creak without a boat, let alone a paddle. A glance of disappointment shot at me from my mother as golden sunlight streamed in through the frosty kitchen windows amidst the white blistering weather.

"We're sorry to come here at this time, Chief."

"You're only doing your jobs gentlemen. Please. Carry on. It's nothing more than id expect in your normal line of duty … tea? Or coffee anyone?"

Both men pulled up their chairs. They removed their hats delicately and placed them upside down upon their laps. They were both huge men, very prodigious in their uniforms, their demeanour professional, their attire very police-like.

"Tea," said one.

"Coffee," said another, and mother played host.

Did I forget to tell you that my father was the Chief of Clitheroe Police. Not that it slipped my mind. He was once Chief of Police of London Metropolitan. He took this job here to be closer to home, and my mother, about the same time I came into their lives. He was a proud man, his life very private, but in all, he had served the public well. He was awarded the congressional medal of honour – twice, due to saving members of the public in a terrorist attack, and latterly for saving six police officers from a blazing building whilst under hostage fire, not to mention being close protection for the royal family.

Both officers glared at me. I was ready for them. "We are here to speak to you, Victor, about last night's trouble at the White Lion Public House.

"O.K," I replied. "How may I help?"

"The man you punched is in intensive care," said the first police officer. "You've broken is bottom jaw in two places. We have been told that late last night he had a metal plate fitted into his left cheek bone."

"He punched me first." I blurted it out in my defence. I was nervous, I guess. There was no way I was being blamed for this. "Both bouncers attacked me head on. I only defended myself." Then empathy struck me at my core. What if he was married with children? What if his wife, partner, was now upset that I'd hurt the one she/he cared for? What if his children saw their father in a hospital bed

riddled with tubes and straws? "Although" I went on, and my face I guess reflected my gestures. "I am sincerely sorr-
..."

"We have seen the CCTV footage." The second officer cut me off bluntly. "You are right. We are not here to arrest you, or to bring prosecution proceedings against you, Victor. We are here simply to ask if you wish to make a charge against both bouncers for their assault upon you first as a valid punter invited into the White Lion Public House?"

I am lost? What were they saying? I think in silence for a short while. "I'm confused," I replied. "But, am I not at fault? I hurt the guy. I knocked him clean out?"

"You did more than hurt him." The voice of the first officer was stern. "However, unknowing how the night would turn out, Victor, he started the trouble, not you. We are aware that he has done this sort of thing with other men your age and has many a time gotten away with it un-scathed," affirmed the officer, bluntly.

"Except this time, *he* came off worse. You hit him only once," finished the second officer, and his eyes fell to my father, as if gratified. "We don't class your actions, con-sidering the state of affairs as an overuse of force. Like you said, Mr Black, you were protecting yourself and protecting your life."

I gave this a long hard think. I felt stunned, my mother glaring at me with solid intention, the likelihood to give me a clout once the Bobbies-in-blue disappeared. Then there was the part about me being immortal. *Or was I dreaming?* My father glares at me with bated opinion linger-ing beneath his breath, an ounce of anticipation looming over my answer. The air about me turns suddenly static. *Was this all really my fault? Am I solely to blame for their ac-tions?* The guy was a bully. In fact, they were both bullies. I sit in silence, my eyes telling a different outcome. A break of yellow sun cracks a white cloud outside above the Hill and the light of our day star shines in on the kitchen table upon my eggs, sunny side up. *Is God hiding in the murky shadows rubbing this in my face?* The officers patiently await my reply as they casually drink their brews and talk police talk in gentle whispers to my father as I sit and contemplate. I was ready now.

"I think he's suffered enough already. I do not wish to press any charges against this man."

"We thought as much," said the first officer, but as he did this he bent down and picked up something sparkly off the kitchen floor. He handed it to my mother. It was a tiny shard of glass. "The last you want is that in your foot, Mrs Whipp."

"Thank you," replied my mother. "God knows how that got there."

"You must have good healing powers, Mr. Black (meaning myself), said the officer. "On CCTV it looked as though you had two black eyes, a fat lip, and a boot mark on your face." The officer glared at me in silence, both of them did. My father bit into his toast. I felt my heart rate fibrillate. It was pounding, and my adrenaline was coursing through my body as if my senses were on overdrive.

"TCP," I said, "with a smell worse than Clitheroe fish markets."

"Indeed," said the first officer with a chuckle.

"That stuff stings like a thousand needles," said the second officer. "I grazed my knee once when I fell off my bike, and my mother put some on my cut. I went through the roof." They both laughed a deep laugh.

"A miracle cure in my opinion," I lied, and smiled.

"That'll be all, Sir," noted the first officer as they both

peered with respect at my father.

"Apologies again, Chief for intruding upon your day off on a Sunday. Thank you for the teas and coffees, Mrs Whipp," added the second officer.

"Anytime officers. Our door is always open," said Ida. They both stood up and placed their hats back upon their heads.

"I would expect nothing less, gentlemen," Robert replied, stoutly. He shook both their hands firmly, as did I. "Enjoy your day gentleman." He said, and he walked them both back to the front door. I heard their car pull off the drive as my father bolted the door back up.

"Let's now have breakfast," he said, and he took his seat across from me, my mother to my right. He appeared rather comfortable in his dressing gown and slippers. I glared at them both, most hard. This was like a stroll in the park to them, but to me it was like a Mexican standoff. They didn't even flinch. *Aren't they going to say something?* After what just happened, there was no way I was tolerating that. I wanted answers, lots of them. I had to push on. I wanted them *now!*

"Hold on." I pulled up my chair. I put my hand up as though traffic control. "What the hell has just gone on?"

"What?" Both Robert and Ida stopped dead.

"It's simple. I'm either told, or I walk right now." I shove my plate in front of me as I deject my food. "I'll pack my things then head back to Scotland. I don't give two hoots if I sleep on a park bench. You two are barking!"

"Is that so," said my father. Then a dark haze filled the room, more than likely the scent of reality hits home for both of them - and for me. He bit down into his toast, and he gave Ida a rather long and gaunt distinguishable look.

"As they say, better late than never." Ida slowly stands then pours out the hot tea as she majestically gives way to my father in dialogue with a subtle glance for him to explain recent events.

"I see," I said slowly, weighing up the situation. *Shall I make a run for it?* I sat there with two people I didn't truly know. I knew that now. "Well?" I was brought up by these two, yet at any time, either of them could've easily killed me at any moment. I mean, what actually where they really? "Who are you both really?"

"*We* are immortal," Robert replied flatly, his voice deep. "You've been told once already by your mother as I was attending the front door. But I will repeat it again, just so it sinks in. *YOU ARE IMMORTAL*" He reached casually forwards for yet another slice of toast (this guy was a bread monster) "There is no easy way to say this, Victor. You are the last bloodline of Sir. William Wallace."

I was dumbfounded. I could've been slapped in the face with a wet chicken fillet and I wouldn't have known. I'm not quite sure how long it was before I answered. I sit and contemplate over this a little longer, a long while longer, I think. I've done that a lot in this chapter, haven't I? Well, when it's a true story, you can't afford to leave no stone unturned. But, eventually, I reached for a piece of bacon off my plate as I gradually unwind my tensive thoughts and come back to my senses. I did not make eye contact with either of them. The bacon was crispy and frazzled, yet stone cold. I didn't see any snow on it. I still ate it, mind. It smelt so good, just like the bouncers' cheeks. They were flabby, and red and pink and rushing with blood. It was also his heart. I remember it was pumping fiercely inside his chest. *The flashbacks were soaring through my mind.* I remember, it was spiked with adrenaline, and that excited me inside. I wanted to open his ribcage and take a bite out of it as though it a bright red apple. I wanted to bite him, all of him, all over, all at once. I wanted to taste his blood, badly. I take a deep sigh. *Maybe I was poorly inside my head? Perhaps I should be in the psyche ward?* There were lots (and lots) running around inside my head at this moment that I wanted to know.

"You are who you are, Victor. That cannot be denied." Ida sipped her tea. She held her cup with two hands, as if to keep them warm.

I best get this ball rolling. Their eyes met mine over the table. "How long have you known I was immortal?" Then it struck me. "In fact, how do you know that I am 'actually' immortal, if at all? I bleed? Do you both bleed? I felt every punch from the doorman last night. I felt my bollocks shoot up into my mouth. I heard my jaw crack. I tasted my own blood, and it was delicious."

"Watch your language, lad," stated my father. "Do not let me tell you again."

Watch my language? The guy is blood sucking – whatever he is. Fuck knows. Anyway, for now, I held my tongue. "I felt my ribs fracture as they both pounded me from left to right like a rugby ball in steal toe cap boots. Isn't it, if a person bleeds, then they can die?"

A hard stone-like glare came from Robert as if grim. He grimaced at Ida, then back to me. He took a deep, thoughtful, breath. I sensed it. The guy was losing it. "You're right, Victor." His gaze was dogged and was followed by a lack of explanation.

"Eat," he nodded to my plate. Ida sat and listened, and drank her mug of tea at slow pace, as if both listening and contemplating her next dialogue.

A flee of bewilderment came over me. Suddenly, my

mother broke down, then got up and turned the heat up for the kettle on the stove, the kitchen drawer opening and closing, pots and pans moving.

I knew something was on her mind. I could see it in her eyes.

"Must we do this now, Robert?" Ida pleaded with my father. "Does it have to be today? Please, Robert?"

"The boy needs to know. This is our way, is it not?"

Ida sobbed, but nodded in silent agreement, though it was upsetting to witness, nonetheless. She began to collect the cups off the table and rinse them at the sink to make a fresh hot pot of tea. She slammed the cups down on the work top. I got a glance of her face as she passed from behind. *What were these people?* Silver tracks of sparkling salt water lined her cheeks. I passed her my napkin, and she took it with glee, and gently caressed my face.

"Arghhh!" Jesus Christ. It went in deep. So, God dam deep.

"Do not use the lord's name in blasphemy, son," my father retorted. "Must I keep repeating myself?"

"Be still my child." Ida drove it down hard.

To say she was a dainty little thing God she was strong. I gripped her arms as she rammed it in even harder. I felt it slice out the back of my ribcage and lodge into the back of my chair. I heard it impale the wood. Four of my ribs cracked in the process. It was thick. *How weird. Words were coming to mind but for some reason I couldn't get them out. I tried to break free from her clutches, but I wasn't able.*

"Be still my little boy ..." she whispered.

"This is great toast, Ida dear. When you're done pour me a hot coffee love."

It was as if a spear of lightening had struck me in the chest. I glared at my father as if for aid, but all he did was eat. I was dying. Then my mother fell to her knees on the kitchen tiles. Out of her came a wallowing scream I had never heard before, not in any woman. It was the cry of loss for a woman's child, as if plucked from her very breasts. It was truly beautiful, yet harrowing to feel its resonance run through you, as if vibrating your bones to the core of life itself. I glared at my mother. Now, she was howling to the moon as if a banshee, the blood of her son on her hands. I slid from off my chair, the pain horrific, yet she caught gently my head from hitting the hard stone floor – *how obscure*. Blood poured out from my chest, pumping at every beat of my fading heart. Its aroma ambient and cherry-sweet it smelt. Hot tears fell from off her cheeks and splashed down onto my forehead.

"The question is, Victor," my father bit yet again into his toast … "Who are you exactly?" He took a hearty sip of his tea. "I asked … who are you?" *Slurp, slurp,* and *slurp.*

Both of them watched on in rigorous scrutiny.

But why? Blood came up to my lips. *Cough. Cough.* I focused in on my last remaining thoughts. And it all began with the tiny splinter of glass on the kitchen floor found by the police officer. I tried to take a deep breath; madness flouted the darker recesses of my thoughts. I was going into shock, but weirdly, a distant image appeared at the thresher of my mind. I brought it back from the very depths of years gone by. It was what my father had said to me that cold November's day as he brought me home for the first time. And I was right. Low and behold! I peeked down. It was there, a mighty black gilded hilt, sparkling white diamonds and rubies as red as blood. It was stuck deep in my chest cavity: *The Black Witch Blade.*

"I took the c-case off the Study wall," Ida sobbed uncontrollably, "… I s-smashed it on the k-kitchen floor. The magic glass from the case cut my skin. I bled for the first time in a thousand years. We did not want you to leave." She cried, and fiercely she wept, sobs of loss and remorse became her worst ally.

Deftly Robert spoke. He came to my side of the table and held my chin as my eyes watered, and the vision of my eyes waned. I glared hard. He said:

"The Athame of Maleficus is yours now, Son … as I promised." He knelt by Ida, he stroked my black wavy locks. And though I tried hard to fight it, the weight of my lids became solid. They were so heavy, so *so* heavy. Warm blood had now filled my lungs. It trickled down and through my insides, running into my stomach, slowly slithering through my airways like the tail end of a long red snake, now cold.

"*…cough.* You're b-both evil…"

Ida's lips caressed my forehead. Robert whispered in my ear. "No, Victor. We are not. Though we have delivered you from evil; nonetheless."

"I will hate you for this forever, Robert Whipp."

"Then so be it." He replied.

I was slipping into abyss. Ida wailed, and her cries of rage scorned the many fields and trees about our home. I heard nesting birds take flight to nearby skies as its echo almost jubilant sounded on the other side of the Ribble Valley.

That voice? It whispered my name, again.

"Victor? Victor!"

Ida's blood stopped weeping. But I was done. The shadow of darkness fell over me as my heart beat its final beat.

"Let's eat breakfast, Ida. It's a shame to waste all this delicious food."

* CHAPTER 7*

~ The Secret Spook ~

I didn't leave the house in what seemed like an age, not after the police had been. I wanted to keep my head low. It was my father's idea; his idea that I stay home and, well – *read:*

"Read what?" I said, but if you ask a silly question, you get a silly answer. That was my first mistake.

"Now that you're very dead, Victor, you will see the world through dead eyes."

What the hell was he talking about? Here we go again with his riddles of life. Honestly, this guy, his whole life, had never stopped surprising me. Always did I listen to him. Always did he keep my mind stimulated. Always, without question, was he there for me, as was mother.

The list of books dropped heavy upon my desk were indeed endless:

The Uncanny, Ovid, and The Interpretation of Dreams – all by the infamous Sigmund Freud, along with the *Three Essays on the Theory of Sexuality. How stimulating.* Then: *The principles of Anatomy and Physiology,* by Tortora and Grabowski (1ˢᵗ Ed); the book could easily have been used as a door wedge at McDonalds. To add to that there was also; *Musculoskeletal, Examination and Assessment,* by Petty and Moore, not to mention, *Classic Human Anatomy in Motion: The Artist's Guide to the Dynamics of Figure Drawing* by Valerie L. Winslow; and *An Anthropology of Anthropology: Is it Time to Shift Paradigms,* by Robert Borofsky, with lastly, quite weirdly, *An Introduction to the Archaeology of Ancient*

Egypt, by Kathryn A. Bard, thus last but not least; *Bottle Digging Adventures: Methods, Techniques and Secrets Revealed* by Steve Homewood & John Brown.

Seriously … was that all? They were piled high. I could even see them in the dark as I lay in bed, night after night.

"For now … there is much you need to learn. Time is of the essence. It's just best not to allow your brain to ruminate on the negative too much, Victor. Study. Study. Study. For if not, your life might depend on it, along with your family."

"But I want answers?" I urged. "Father, please?"

"In time," he said, "all will be revealed."

Outstanding – although, it made my mother feel better, me being home. It wasn't easy, not after you're told that you're an immortal, and then you're stabbed in the chest from high above by the only woman that was supposed to care for you. I have a scar now, though I'm told only other immortals can see it. The blade left its mark alright, along with its sigil, all over my freaking body: it starts in the middle of my sternum, a full blood moon above a tall wood with three black witches stirring their cauldron afire, their black cat watching. I mean, what sort of crazy shit was this? I stand naked in my bedroom mirror, glaring at it, trying to understand its path, its riddles, its mayhem. I have Pendle Forest in dense trees, and the Hill etched upon my back, the deep Glens of my homeland, Scotland scribed in electric-white and emerald-green flashings of ink, red skies, Smilodon wolves lurking in dark crevices filtered through with orange and pink clouds. I'm surprised there wasn't a fluffy fucking rainbow lurking. But both my arms carry Sir. William Wallace's swords, both scribed in his name, blood-ridden. Their silver glitters abundantly as excess light from my curtains catches the two handled claymores. Except, it won't wash off. Bleach doesn't work, though it smells like hell, but not as bad as TCP. *I think I'm scared by the yellow piss.* Yet when I awoke from my stabbing, I felt no pain. I felt as though I was in a dream. Life and the senses about me had magnified tenfold. I reminisce a little more as I lay in bed, awake, but dozing. Little to my knowledge, my father had other things planned for me. I could hear the birds begin their dawning songs, fluttering from tree to tree.

"UP!" shouted a dim voice.

Did I hear that right? The rose in my tinted spectacles had just about cracked. I have no other explanation for it. It was barely breaking dawn; the sun was hiding to the east as it rested beneath the immense plush horizon of Pendle Hill.

What the hell? "Pardon?" I shout to the dark. "Wha – who - who is it?"

It was a dull grey Saturday morning. I was met with soft flakes of pure white snow as I opened my bedroom curtains. The top of Pendle Hill was in speckles of white mist and grey shadow against the dark back drop of the sunlit horizon wreathed amidst its very peak in yellow. It was 06.00am. I didn't know it but that day was the very start of my career. I awoke to the sound of my father's voice ascending the stairwell as I stood at my window smelling the cold damp air. There was a scent on the wind, but what it was, I did not know.

"GET UP VICTOR!"

I could feel my decorum slipping beneath the very arches of my feet as though skating on thin ice. I was seriously unsteady underfoot. There was no way I would cross this man; polite and graceful as he may be, his aspirations over the years brandished with a cast-iron surety not even

"Are you taking the piss?" I front Ivan squarely, black belt or not. He lowers his hand. "For years you bullied me." I poked him hard in the chest and knocked him back. "You *are* my enemy." There was a sparkle of respect in his eyes, a buzz of unsurity in the air. His father gave an acknowledged response of hardened dignity to my father. I felt he was impressed with what he had borne witness too. Ivan stepped back towards me at the nod of his father, nose to nose. He then spoke again.

"For years I have prepared you." This he said with a sense of pride, almost as if he felt chosen at being given this task to complete, which he was. His voice was monotone, his nature completely placid. I felt then he had a stout heart. I felt then his sense of premise strong.

Would he really have helped that night if the bouncers were getting the better of me? Was this all an act? "Prepared me? Do you know how suicidal you made me? Have you any idea, Ivan?" I side glanced my father. "Did you know about this? Is this some sort of sick joke?"

His sense was diminished. Beaten. Depraved. Riddled in guilt. I could almost taste it. *Was this his mistake?* It seemed he held silence for some time; his lips tighten as he shows a pout of pre-planned misconception. Then, Robert said:

"I was the one that ordered it."

Ouch. I bet that fucking hurt.

"Though I am often plagued with my decision. It haunts me to this day. I have been regretting this day, yet also awaiting its coming," he said.

I stepped back dumbfounded. I fell almost, my footing loose. "O-ordered it?" Inside my ribs burst with cryptic bouts of adrenaline. I felt my bones crack with a sense of hostility. A new hollowness appeared beneath the essence of my being, my conception, my qualified rights. I felt un-dignified. Used. Manipulated. "This was a set up – a complete and utter fucking set up - *all* this time? Are you the Three Stooges?"

Mr. Vray Snr, Mr Vray Jnr, and my father pass a look of absence to the other, with neither, yet all, failing to take full responsibility.

"I did not want to fight you Victor outside the White Lion. Your discovery of my presence took me by surprise. I wore a black cap and hid at the back of the crowds. I was there to fight with you and watch over your safety. Those I was with I told to vacate my person. They too are students at this school. I had to back down and allow you to supersede my presence. I acted like a coward. I had to sympathise with your better nature."

I become fixed at the mere concept of their formulated deception. *This was clearly a group effort, or my name was Bilbo Baggins of the Shire.* I fight the urge not to hurt this man. He was a sneak. "Super – sed, -wha?" I pause for what seemed like a while to make sense of the madness. I swear if there was a seat next to me I'd've sat right on it and allowed a big black hole to swallow me whole. *What the hell would my mother say to all this palaver?* I know. "Are you all sick in the head?" It just slipped off my aggravated tongue. What else was I led to believe?

"I like this kid, Bob." Mr. Vray Snr seemed to smirk at the comment, my father of his opinion flashes a small wink.

"You have been prepared, Victor." Ivan Vray Jnr cited. "I am the one responsible for your emotional, psychological, and environmental well-being. I was chosen. I was proud to help bring your immortality into fruition. I agreed to this quest. It is a pleasure to meet you at last." He held out his hand.

"I have been lied to, father. All this time here, you, mother, it was all a god dam lie!" The better part of my sensibility was losing grip on reality. I was going to smack this fucker any moment. The cheek of it.

"Do not use the lord's name in blasphemy."

"God has nothing to do with this. When I died I didn't see any white light. No angels came for me on that day, let me tell you. Oh no. I was alone, while you and mother continued to eat breakfast in my absence. I am surprised you didn't choke on it."

He shot me a harsh glare filled with concrete stones. The muscles in the side of his jaw glistened against the lights of the church foyer. The wind in the trees outside howled, a glimpse of headstones enters my view as a search for a quick exit lingers in my vision. Instantly, but on for a mere moment, I changed my mind.

I spat. "Fuck the lord. Where was *he* at my birth? Where was *he* when I was beaten black and blue at the orphanage for merely asking for more food? Where was *he* when I fell as a boy? ..."

Without hesitation he fronted me sharply. The dragons were back again. I stepped back a tad. Both Ivan's moved slowly apart. *Aren't their feet getting cold? Shall I stand on Ivan's toes?* We were in late November, it was pissing with snow, yet in their suits they seemed as warm as toast. *Bloody idiots.* He raised a single hand, his finger pointing harshly. "None of it was a lie, Victor. You came to us an orphan. You were being hunted by the Black Knights." Then he said something that I will never forget. "The man on the train was my father. He was the only man I could ever trust to transport you from Midlothian to here. He was under specific instruction to deliver you to me. *Only to me!*"

Bare-knuckle Bob? "Bu-…"

"That was his final mission," he said. Both Ivan's became blessed, and said, "Amen," at Bobs name, and showed the sign of the crucifix. *What the hell?*

"His middle name was Victor." He was my best friend." He lowered his hand. His face changed, his eyes a watery haze of blue at his next comment. "We had to kidnap you, to save you lad. None of us wanted to take you away from the orphanage." The wind through the wooden doors howled. A drift of white snow blew in. "But in all the lies, and all the deceit to keep you safe, to bring your senses into fruition, I am glad we did."

"Amen to that," said both Ivan Snr, and Ivan Jnr in chorus.

I listen for any kind of regret in his voice. There was none. But I had to know. "Where is Bob now?" The fluttering of my heart skipped a beat. "You never told me." *This man was my saviour. He was the one who broke bread with me despite it riddled with coal dust.* All I can think about right now was discovering the truth. The whole truth. Nothing but the truth. I felt almost slave to it. There was an overwhelming sense of injustice that shod heavy over every orifice of my epidermis, as if magnified tenfold. I watched as my father almost broke down. I bore witness to it. A scolding pain welled in my chest.

"We don't know. Our intel has never known."

"Our intel?" I was curious.

"We are independent of any military organisation or special investigations branch, but are subject to a secret group, one governed by our government that has survived for over five centuries."

"Secret government?"

"We are of the Royal Immortal Charter, a higher

governmental authority. But more about that another time."

I could tell he was keen to finish his tale. "Continue."

"When the train pulled into Blackburn Station, he simply wasn't on it. That's all we knew. Word on the ground was he had vanished into thin air. Literally. In all, the day before you arrived; that was the last we ever saw of him. My search for him since has been in vain. Now, he doesn't exist. He's just a ghost."

"We?" I'm a little perplexed. "Who is we?" I am calm, though Ivan Jnr had moved back out of arms reach. I still reckon I can take him - kung-fu Charlie. Ill tie his pyjamas around his freaking neck.

My father glanced to Ivan Snr.

"What? Chewbacca here?" I reply.

"Easy young-en," remarked Ivan snr.

Somehow, he didn't seem that impressed at my sarcasm, though I had guessed that he and his son were part of the higher government squad. I pointed at him in such a way it must've pissed him right off. Ivan Jnr sniggered. It didn't go down well with old tall pops at all. "Is your middle name, Bob by any chance?" I was fuming.

"Listen laddie ..." Here came the deep Scottish accent. He towered over me. This guy was huge. How come I'd never seen him walking around Clitheroe before? I mean, you couldn't miss him. He was like a walking lamppost. He glared hard but serenely at me. He edged a little closer. I look up, unflinching. There was a dark abyss that went beyond the far reaches of his soul. I saw that now. He had dragons in his closet to. I felt it. "My kill record might not be as high as your fathers, but I killed my enemies with my bare hands, nonetheless."

Goosebumps begin to rise on the back of my neck.

Kill record? Ivan backs off, his arms folded. We glared for a while, all of us at all of us, an eerie silence drew up like the breath of satin. There was more I wanted to know. Then I ask over an old memory, one that's haunted me ever since. "The inscription scribed upon his silver pocket watch - what was it?"

"You saw his watch?" There was a bolt of enlightenment that shimmered over my father's face. He relished in the thought of being asked that very question. I could feel it deep in the roots of my hair. "You have a good memory. I was their when it was gifted to him. It read, ""To my beautiful husband and father ... all my love, Leanne.""

"Leanne?"

His stare was ardent. "I have never spoken of her previously. Leanne was my mother. She passed long before your arrival: *KIA*."

I take a deep sigh. "I often wondered over the watch." I shake my head in pity. "But why?" I asked. "Why the bullying? Why the torment?" Ivan eyed me, as if with regret. "Why now am I integrated into this secret order of plant pots?"

"Plant pots?" remarked Ivan Jnr. "What have plants pots to do with this moment in time?"

"I am not proud of what I am about to tell you. But put simply. It was to save your life," said my father.

"I didn't need my life saving." I reply harshly.

"This is the problem. You do. You had to be made to feel isolated. You had to be made to feel alone. You had to be made to feel abandoned, by peers, friends, and family. To experience that experience was for you to experience that very experience. Nothing more. To merely absorb the negativity of your environment, the smell of your own fear, the call of your inner world, was but to drive your emotions as high as possible. We had to reach into the very depths of your soul in hope for you succeed at whatever it was that you put your mind too. Failure, Victor, is not an option. Not in this life. Not anymore."

"Why?"

"We only learn how to survive by hurtful emotion. It builds drive. It builds inner character. It hardens the soul and frees your aspirations in a bid to escape your burdens, but to prove your worth to others, even if to yourself. Without doubt it drives instinctual survival in the competitiveness of life itself. And this alone is priceless," said my father overtly. "This, for us immortals, is the only way. Life is bitterly unfair."

I'd never heard my father speak with such tenacity, such critical analysis of one's own being. *The guy had a serious screw loose. That was one big head mash. What the hell?* They all see. I think about running out the doors and up onto the fells of Pendle. Or perhaps pull up a chair outside the Wellsprings Inn at the Nick o' Pendle and take refuge beneath the measure of a few golden pints of ale, drown my sorrows as I glare out over the Ribble Valley, the Castle in the far distance bolstering the colours of the St George flag of England. *How fucked up was this?* I'll sit with the snowmen and freeze off my marbles. Or better still; wander off over The Hill never to return. Perhaps in time people will see me as the Werewolf of Pendle. Maybe someday I'll join in the tales of folklore of the Pendle Witches. *Fuck knows.* They watch me in awe. They wait.

Ivan Jnr, Ivan Snr, and my father, both take off their clothes in the foyer. They strip naked, right down to their waists.

"What are you all doing?" I stand well back. "Put it away, man!"

"This way you will see our marks, Victor. We are not your enemies, but are in fact your allies. Even your family,"

Taken aback, I'm mesmerised. Their skin glowed in fantastic yet psychedelic colours as a thin spear of sunlight broke the seal on nearby glass leaded windows of the church. All their immortal marks were much different from my own – each and every one of them.

"Do you see now, Victor?" said my father. As he rotated, amidst his back, a large wolfs head laid bare, a Black Alpha, its pack running below; rivers and ice-capped mountains; his chest a pure white nun, her rosemary crucifix in tow, his arms embossed with black arrows, white flights, silver nibs, its bow strongly resting across his shoulders, his neck pounding with blue sapphires ridden over the lashing tail of a green dragon, his abdomen riddled with images of all thirteen anthems. "I am the Gate Keeper to the Underworld", he said.

What the fuck was the Underworld? "I don't follow?"

"I too am in liege with your father, for he is our Alpha", retorted Ivan Snr, a white polar bear, huge in stature just like the man himself, its teeth snarling, its claws ever sharp scribed upon his back; the mightiest of eagles, open winged, bare upon his chest, three flighty mongooses across his shoulders, his neck riddled with pure white diamonds, his arms flecked with the bows of three mighty oaken trees, his abdomen a wise owl of ancient times. He affirmed openly: "I am the protector of the Gate Keeper."

"Take me!" exclaimed Ivan Jnr; his chest bore a Viper, venomous and lean, his back the image of a great red-fire amidst a deep green forest, yet beneath it, two yellow eyes looked out, its body unseen; his neck a reflection of thorns, black and sharp, his arms white doves adorned his skin, his shoulders that of an Indian Chief, the feathers long and coloured and draping. "I am a warrior of the Fire-spirit." Ivan jnr confessed. "I am the protector of the Hunter."

There came at last a halt to the display of their sigil's, and I felt the history of their telling's indeed tended for. We all stood motionless in wonder. But after a short bout of silence, eventually, the silence gets to me.

"What now?" Things couldn't get any worse, let's face it. I was stood with two elite killers and one boy I thought was a bully whose father beat on him but now he is not a bully but Clitheroe's finest fucking actor with streaks of fire strewn upon his back. Give the guy an Oscar. *Why not?* He's fucking earned it. Nearly 24 months of shite he gave me in his attempt to coax out of me my unbridled ferocity. *Seriously*? Internally, I think he secretly enjoyed it. Shit like this only happens on EastEnders for Christ's sake.

"I would understand if you wanted to leave never to return." That must have hurt as my father said that. Both Ivan's glared staunchly as each of them got dressed. There was loyalty in their stead to the man I call my dad. Each was in anticipation at my next move, all three of them a nervous audience awaiting my answer. I could their heart-beats go up a notch, as if with anticipation. "Though should that be your wish, Victor, it will surely break you mother's heart." He added.

Was he trying to blackmail me? That's right, pull on my heartstrings. "I see," I said.

"You need to learn how to fight. I am told the Black Knights to this day still await your return. They have never given up searching for you." He moved away from the door. In broached more silver daylight, the winds of winter incoming.

I could smell freedom upon my lips, taste the air of

fine virtuosity as if a great weight had been lifted from me. "Mother's heart, eh? ... Black Knights?" I glare at the door, then back at the man who had been my father for the best part of two decades - the Police Chief: *the Immortal*. I realised then my whole life had been based on lies. *What a joke.* As I glared into the depths of the church, its hard wooden beams bearing down strength from above, the statue of our Lord in full view, the other students were still regimentally sat cross-legged and unmoving. *Where they completely simple? Why would someone do such a thing?*

"They'll not move lad." It was Chewbacca. "That's discipline. That's life the Martial Way."

I put my hands in my pockets so they could see I had no intention of starting any trouble. I turn to my father. "This is one serious head fuck." Let's face facts – if Chewbacca got a hold of me he'd tie me up in knots. My head flashes back to over a decade ago whilst on holiday in Torquay at the cinema in town. I try and make sense of the situation. Mr Ivan Snr strongly reminded me of the villain, *Jaws* from *James Bond*, except without the metal teeth.

"If you accept to stay, then you must train here daily in order to learn the ways of mixed martial arts. It is an assassin's key weapon to survival. Mr. Ivan Fray will be your instructor. He is well versed in single armed and unarmed combat, along with samurai and other fighting weapons."

"I see," I nod. *Was this guy for real?*

In essence, keenly, my father awaited my answer. To be honest, I think both the Ivan's did too. I still wanted to smack Ivan Jnr in the mouth and knock all his teeth to the back of his throat. *Shall i?* All their heartbeats were now shallow; there was no adrenaline about them, not like when I first walked in, mainly Ivan Jnr.

"I too will help, Victor." Ivan Jnr seemed sincere, but

was it all an act? "I am sorry for the part I played. But they made me do it." He pointed as if telling tales at my father, blaming also his own father. "Ask them. It's all their fault."

"What of my anthropology degree?"

"I have spoken with a Spook in York who also runs classes. You will attend his classes during term time whilst you're studying at York St John College."

"His name?"

"His name is Steven King…"

"…the author?"

"…not the author. This Spooks nickname is Nytemare. You will see why when you read his sigils for they are embossed with the Grim Reaper, Jackals and Rats. But whilst here, when home, you will train here. I anticipate that you will achieve black belt in less than three months. Steven is an amazing instructor. He has trained with the Shaolin Monks and knows many of their hidden secrets. He is 900 years old, give or take a year or two, and is a well-oiled veteran of warfare."

Is this guy pulling my leg? If Steven is 900, then how old is my father? Mother too come to think of it.

"You are immortal now, Victor. You have your whole life ahead of you. You will learn at greater speed, you will research academia faster, retain knowledge deeper than any human, and recite it with stealth, and high accuracy."

Is that possible? "Then what?"

He put his hand on my shoulder. "Then you will be initiated into our Order," said my father.

"Not for me it's not," I replied in haste. I refuted this offer. "I'm not a killer like you guys. Crawling around in the bush and heading off to foreign countries with huge desserts and worn torn buildings is not my cup of tea. I can't help you with that. It's far too dangerous for my liking."

"That's a shame." He was serious. My father didn't jest. "Unless you train to fight, you could be targeted at any time, yet at the moment your location is secret. You will be trained with sword and shield, bow and arrow, ball and chain, net and spear."

Nope. Not for me." I begin to get ready to leave. "This is all hocus pocus crap."

"You're still being hunted. Every day they hunt you. The Black Knights. They will stop at nothing to take you from your family. They will stop at nothing to kill your family. Kill us all. In their eyes you are their idol. In their eyes you, Victor, are their re-born King … their leader sent from the Great Witch God: Samhain.

Witch God? I thought. I couldn't help it.

Mr Vray Snr seemed embellished yet sincere in his own achievements. He pointed to those sat cross-legged on the Main Hall floor. "All those you see here are part of our Order," he reiterated. "I only train secret spooks. They are like us. Period. My endearing mission is to train those that have the ability to kill. To train those just like you."

Ivan shrugs his shoulders as if he's got no part to play in that comment.

"There are other immortals in Clitheroe?" I asked.

"There are other immortals all over England, Scotland, Wales, and Ireland. Yet once there were many. Now there are only few."

"I have requested through your lecturer on campus that you attend additional physiotherapy lectures in your spare time, both theoretical and practical, "stated my father. "I have paid for this privilege. After all, education is a business, right?"

"… and?"

"She has agreed."

"Physiotherapy? Bu-" *Was this guy for real?* "I need to rest in-between lectures. I can't just go and learn another degree as well as already doing one degree."

"You're not listening, Victor. What are the bones of the hand? Quickly now. Recite the information for me."

"Scaphoid, lunate, triquetral, pisiform, trapezium, trapezoid, capitate, hamate." *What the shit? Did I just say that?* "Where the hell did that come from?"

"See ... yes you can. It'll help with your Latin. It'll help with becoming more familiar with your anatomy and physiology. It'll help you become a better more lethal killer. But it will also help you become a healer. We don't kill for the sake of killing. We kill to protect the innocent. We kill those that oppose us. We kill those that want to cover the world in darkness."

I stand gaunt looking. I say nothing in return. To me, they were asking the impossible. *Sack this shit.* They just weren't taking no for an answer. At that precise point there was an inkling of subdued submission that oozed out from me. *Just go with it*, I thought. *For now.* I glared about the Hall. *Could I really be a killer? Would my life truly end if the Black Knights discover my identity?*

"If you fail to fight, then we are left to fight on your behalf. We are aware that the Black Knights are all secret spooks. They are a religious cult, and come from beyond The Witch Quarry Gate, the entrance to the Underworld. We don't know who they are exactly, Victor. They are like us in lots of ways, but in many, not so. We also may be assassinated. Your mother too. There is a possibility they had something to do with my father's disappearance ..." He paused momentarily "... and also my mother's death. We don't truly know."

What a day it's turned out to be. I confront my dae-mons, all my hard work seemed to pay off. I'm thrown out of bed at the crack of dawn; I meet Chewbacca and Clit-heroe's best actor, and now this? It was clear the gates of oblivion had most certainly come for me, to shackle me in a void of despair alongside Lucifer, to hold me down until I admit defeat. This guy wanted his pound of flesh. *Let's hope he didn't spill a drop of my blood in the meantime.*

"Are you with us, Victor?"

It came to me. "I'm done. I can't do this. Sorry. I'll head back to Scotland to live a peaceful life. I'll finish University and find a good job, settle down and god willing start a family. There has to be some lucky lady out there for me." I turn for the door.

"We immortals are obsolete in the eyes of the nor-mal world. To humans, we don't exist. We are folklore, tales of old, myths by scholars once but now long forgotten."

"This is very true," repeated Ivan Snr. "We do not have the same abilities as you. You are able to read minds, hear heart beats, and you have the ability to move at the speed of light. That type of 'gift' has only ever been seen in Sir. William Wallace. He too an immortal, with God has his witness."

"Without you on side, we are blind." Ivan Jnr held out his hand again. "Forgive me of my actions. Farewell, Victor. May God speed you, and may always enjoy spa-ghetti?" He joked.

"You should start acting school," I fly a swift com-ment of sarcasm back. "You're not just good. You're dam good." I open the door, the sun blinkers my view. I step over its thick wooden thresher. I am free at last.

"You're the only one, Victor, that can find my father," stated my father. "You are the only one with that ability."

Bare knuckle Bob? I stop dead. I take a deep sigh. *How fucking pedantic. He had me by the bollocks. This was the guy that broke bread with me. He saved my life. He cleared my air-ways. I took his first name in his memory.* Thinking deep, I didn't want to admit it, but I had a debt to repay. It was true. There was no question of it. I turn back to face all three. "Should any of you piss me off again, or lie to me, I walk. Get it?"

"We do," they said in chorus.

Am I doing the right thing? Fuck knows. "When do I begin?"

"Now, Victor," replied my father. "If the Black Knights obtain all Thirteen Witch Blades, it will bring our world in to an apocalypse of biblical proportion. You must not let not even one blade fall into their hands, Victor."

Ivan Vray Jnr held out his hand (yet again). "Well?" He smiled, as if all was forgiven. Not. "I offer you my friendship, Victor."

Was this guy an idiot? "Fuck you - muppet," though a harsh jest, I think he got the message.

"Once you are ready, Egypt will be your first port of call. Ivan Jnr will go with you," clarified my father.

"Egypt? … with the actor?"

"Now is not the time for disagreements, Ivan." He nodded at Ivan Snr. "But is indeed the right time for new beginnings."

"New beginnings?" I become paranoid. *Was someone going to stab me again?*

Ivan Snr reached then pulled a lever on the wall hidden by an old bookshelf "Hold on Victor," said Ivan Snr. "Now we take you to our world."

"Muppet?" repeated Ivan Jnr. "What the hell does a

muppet have to do with the price of bread?" He seemed confused and scratched his head.

"Human weapons such as guns, RPG's, claymore mines, hand grenades do not work against the immortals," Ivan Snr quoted. "Though they will work against other humans should their services be yoked by them. Adding to that, the weapons you will use against the immortals are specially made of bright drawn silver, some doused in magic, others fashioned in the old ways by the Weapon Smiths beyond the Quarry Gate.

"Outstanding," I replied. *Who was this guy – Gandalf?*

"There are two worlds here, Victor: their world, and our world. The Athames you now seek could be anywhere." Robert said it with a tad of ferocity, which was how I took it.

The whole floor of the church started to descend below the earth.

"What the fuck?" I whispered.

BOOK 2

COMING SOON